Book Four
Found Tales of Northborough

Renee M. Kenny
Portraits of Captain Brendan by Axelle Girard
Cover art by Axelle Girard

Table of Contents

Prologue Page 4

Book I   A Dog for a Cup

P. 5

Book II Leisure for Rights

P. 15

Book III   A Stranger for a Princess

P. 28

Book IV A Fairy for a Cup

P. 36

Book V A Journey for a Captain

P. 47

Book VI An Unlikely Friendship

P. 60

Book VII A Dilemma for a King

P. 71

Book VIII Power for Warmth

P. 85

Book IX Rights for a Princess

P. 103

Book X A Chance for Happiness

P 113

This book is dedicated to my family. Thank you for everything.

Prologue

I knew I wasn't going to live forever. Yes, there are magical spells, which, I think, can *prolong* life, but no one lives forever. Not in Northborough, at least. So I wrote down the stories, wrote them down and hid them. You know, I now live at the Church of the Holy Sandal, and there is a little box where the parishioners put their offerings, but it has a false bottom. I hid my manuscript there. I don't know if anyone will ever read these words, but I hope they do. I hid it from the Druids, for you never know. I have always tried to straddle both the old and new religions, and it's not easy pleasing everyone! I had to be really careful with my lovely mistress Rhiannon.

Oh, and I changed my name, too. Didn't think that anyone would read a story by someone by the name of Goslar. Instead, I used a fancy *nom de plume*, an elegant Gaulish name to write these stories. It's a little way to remember me, and the miraculous things and interesting people whom I have seen and known. Thank you for taking up this manuscript; I'm glad you found it. Perhaps you can say a little prayer for my soul as you do, and I'll thank you.

Book I

A Dog for a Cup

Chapter One

Standing alone in the forest, Morag let the wind tease her hair. She bent down, spying one of the little edible mushrooms she loved. Gathering food from the forest was usually illegal, since the king owned all forest land. However, she had been given a dispensation, as she lived alone, no man to help her (in the eyes of the law, women were pretty helpless). Morag still gave her fair share of her crops to the royal family, but treats like this perfect round, light greyish mushroom, kept her going. She placed it in the basket she balanced upon her left arm.

Not much had changed in her life. After her parents both died, she kept their cottage neat and tidy. She farmed and cooked for herself and her beloved dog, Montgomery, a regal name for a foundling mutt. He had just shown up one day, a gift of the fates; she took him in, assuming he was some kind of mixed breed. Monty made up for his ugliness, for his shaggy hair and loopy legs, for his mixture of colors, with undying loyalty to Morag. She was certain that he kept her sane, as she spoke to him like a sibling, child or friend, which he was, in fact, a combination of for her.

Monty slept at the foot of her bed, barked just to hear the sound of his voice, and appreciated the food she gave him. Her constant companion, he was always up for a walk or just an evening spent resting by the fireplace. What a good-natured lad he was, thought Morag. She doubted that she would ever meet a human as good as Monty. It seemed unlikely, as she lived in a remote area of Northborough and had learned independence by necessity.

Morag's brother Ranaulf, as a toddler, had betrayed her by drinking from the dragon's cup. Their mother Matilda had repeatedly told him not to. "No, No No!" she warned, wagging her finger at its evil visage. The cup had been their only family heirloom. Matilda never forgave herself for keeping it. She had stored it up on the mantelpiece, out of Ranaulf's reach, but one day, when the cats played their game of "catch," a swishing tail brushed upon the pewter cup, bringing it to the earth. It fell right into baby Ranaulf's lap. Naturally, with the curiosity of a child, he poured himself a drink of water. Immediately, his head spun and he became very dizzy. The boy woke up in Caradon Hall, the main castle of Northborough, where the king and family lived. There, the ladies-in-waiting clamored over his beauty, wanting to keep him, almost like a pet. Luckily, just then Queen Aurelia descended the stairs from her solar. Believing him to be a gift, she ordered the ladies and nurses to raise Ranaulf like a prince, as if he were born there.

Years later the queen gave birth to a boy herself, but this child bore a mark on his cheek. The sorcerer in the turret high above them decided that the mark meant little Rory was cursed, so asked Ranaulf to take him to the forest and bury him in the snow.

Ranaulf could do no such thing, so he killed a rabbit for its blood, brought the crimson-stained swaddling clothes to the magician, and claimed that a wolf had killed the baby. Ranaulf found another cottage, where a wilderness couple, Julian and Anne, agreed to raise the child in secret.

Queen Aurelia's husband, older and sickly, did not survive the supposed death of his only son and heir. So the sorcerer's brother ruled, not very kindly, and the people wanted to revolt. The former Duke of Malverne raised taxes to support his lavish lifestyle. The people found their ruler in Rory, whose stepfather revealed to him his identity. Rory raised a small army to challenge King Medard, but when he arrived at the castle, the knights recognized his birthmark and would not fight. They crowned him the rightful king, putting Medard, the sorcerer, and Malverne, the king, into jail for life.

Morag had heard of all of this, naturally. Most of Northborough's citizens met on Sundays for Mass, so she knew of her brother's rise, and resented it. Not everyone believed in the new religion, Christianity, named for the followers of Jesus Christ, but they liked seeing each other once a week and hearing what Brother Bede had to say. Jesus had lived, died, and then lived again in Palestine many years ago. He cured leprosy, brought the dead back to life, and fed thousands with a few loaves and fishes. If true, He was a powerful magician indeed. More powerful than anyone in Northborough, as far as she knew. She had heard of Merlin's powers, and Morgan le Fay's, too. This Christ seemed to be even more powerful than they.

But this new sect did not really focus on the miracles, but on human kindness, humility and generosity. Morag herself had been raised a pagan, as her parents had feared the power of the Druids and others who practiced the dark arts. Morag had time to think about these things, and she decided that she may as well give allegiance to both groups. She did not want to anger either side, so she went to church, and respected the old ways, as well. The Druids had the knowledge of centuries; they produced madness on command; they uttered frightening incantations. Druids brewed noxious beverages that interrupted or destroyed the mind; she knew better than to tangle with that. Which is why she had the sense never to touch the Cup.

While Ranaulf lived in the splendor of a castle, becoming page, squire and then knight, she nursed her mother and father in their old age. She buried them in the land around the cottage, and mourned them alone. Their father had taught her farming; their mother the arts of the kitchen and sewing. She did not need anyone, she told herself over and over again. Loneliness, her companion, hurt, but Monty helped.

Then one day Ranaulf appeared at her doorstep. What a surprise. She truly hoped that she didn't treat him rudely, it was just hard to be nice. She had offered him food and drink, and they talked. The awkwardness between them felt like a fog. Morag realized their resemblance; they were unmistakably siblings. Ranaulf, the star, the darling of the court, left and she had not seen him again. She realized that she could not completely blame him for what happened, as the dark magic in the cup was meant to cause trouble, and it had. At least the king at the time, Rory, benefited from having Sir Ranaulf around, as he was now called.

Morag heard that Ranaulf had fallen in love with the ex-queen, Clothilde. That figures! He always prefered royalty to commoners. Even the new king, Dylan, called him "uncle." Perhaps he cannot be blamed for his bourgois nature given that he was raised in a castle along with princesses. Perhaps even Morag would act like a blueblood in that situation, but she doubted it. "If I sound bitter," she told Monty, "I am. But what is to be done but live each day as it comes?" My brother has built a church, an everlasting structure to honor him, and no one will ever forget Sir Ranaulf. Soon they will be calling him "*Saint* Ranaulf"! I have been forgotten already, by everyone except Monty, of course, she mused.

Her basket nearly full, Morag began strolling toward the coast. This was her second cottage, Maud and Hugh having moved after the disappearance of baby Ranaulf. Maud never forgave herself for keeping the cup. She prayed every day for Ranaulf's safety, not realizing that he was near and also living a life of luxury. Hugh felt terrible for not protecting his son. His son resembled his beautiful wife Matilda, and he thanked the gods. Morag called out to Monty, whose favorite thing in the world was splashing in the water. He did not care if he shook his fur out next to Morag, getting her soaked, but nor did she. They stood at the beach, where it became even windier. The surf had picked up. Her blond braids whipped across her face, and as she turned from the wild sea, she noticed someone standing near her, to her right.

Chapter Two

Morag shook with fright, as no one had been standing there a second ago. *What dark magic is this*, she wondered. After what had happened with Ranaulf, she wanted nothing to do with the world of witchcraft.

"Hail, Morag," the woman said, whose skin, hair, nails and gown all gleamed shades of lilac, reflecting the wonder of the ocean. Morag knew that this was no ordinary woman. The apparition wore sprigs of lilac in her hair. Her movements were regal, like a queen's. Even her voice sounded special, musical and cadenced unlike her own. Morag narrowed her eyes. *I am not stupid*, she said to herself. *I know not to mingle with magic.*

"Hello, fair lady. How are you this day?" Morag asked.

"Well, thank you, but I am here for a reason and have no time for small talk. I noticed that your brother once possessed a very special vessel, a cup, made of pewter, crafted centuries ago by women like me. It had been handed down, generation after generation, to the eldest daughter in your family. You, Morag, are that daughter, and I want that cup."

Just as she was about to respond, Morag looked to her left. There stood another wispy apparition, this one a vision in shades of green. The woman wore an olive green gown and pine branches in her hair. She checked to make sure that Monty still played nearby; in fact he was in the shallows, running back and forth with the tide, oblivious. But then he heard the women's voices, and, worried, he came to her side. Monty barked at the women. Morag stood terrified as the second one spoke.

"Hail, Morag. How are you today? My name is Branwen, and I'm Rhiannon's sister. Surely you remember Rhiannon?"

"I do, lady." there was much church gossip when the beautiful blue woman died, after trying to resurrect her beloved King Rory. Her botched witchcraft led to her son's losing his legs. Morag knew to fear this meddling with the natural way of things.

"And I am called Cigfa," the mauve woman added. "I am also the sister of Rhiannon and Branwen. We miss our dear sister so much. There is not much to do at court anymore. We, naturally, are members of the Court of Magical Society. Not that you would know, but it is the premier club that anyone can belong to. We don't let in just anyone. We play games, dance, and have more fun than you can imagine. But lately we have had nothing to do. Once you beat everyone in chess and at cards, the challenge vanishes. That's why we're here."

"Yes, Morag. Do not be surprised that I know your name. I have a telling ball, in which I can see everything that goes on in Northborough. I watch you, and have been wondering where you have hidden the Enchanted Cup. Do not look surprised. Your brother came back, we know. He came back because he had the cup. He came back to your cottage. He talked with you and then he left. But he no longer possesses the cup. Where have you hidden it?" Branwen inquired, kindly, trying to draw her in.

"Tell us nicely, and we will leave you alone. We need diversions. Having the Enchanted Cup at court would mean new adventures all the time. It could relieve our boredom. So tell us, fair Morag, what you've done with it." Cigfa glanced at Monty, and Morag felt a chill go through her bones. Monty growled at Cigfa.

"I wish that I could tell you, dear ladies, where it has gone. But that is not how the cup works; when one drinks from it, they fall into a trance and lose power over their limbs. They drop the cup-- and now it is gone. I have no idea where it is, honestly, and I am sorry."

Branwen looked at her sister. Together they nodded, and then Monty, a second ago frolicking in the surf, stiffened and fell over. Morag screamed and ran to him. She bent down and began petting her beloved dog. "Monty, Monty, are you all right? Please respond!" She frantically kept rubbing his motley fur, to no avail.

"Oh, so sorry that we had to do that. If you keep lying to us, your ugly dog will suffer."

"I'm NOT lying! I don't know where that cursed cup is, and I don't care, either. And don't call my dog 'ugly'!" Morag responded.

"Look, Morag. We did that to show you we're not messing around. If you respond that way, the mutt will die," warned Cigfa.

With that, Monty's body lifted into the air and began spinning in a circle. Morag screamed, "Stop it! Stop it!" She ran to the left and right, but right through Cigfa and Branwen, who were merely apparitions. They just laughed at her.

"So are you ready, now, to tell us where you've hidden the enchanted cup? Or do we have to drop little puppy-poo and see if he breaks?"

"No! Do not drop him! I'll find the cup! I will find it, I promise! Just don't hurt Monty!" she pleaded with them.

Monty slowly gravitated to the sand. The two women disappeared, just like that. Morag ran to her canine friend, petting him and speaking to him softly. "There, there, sweet Monty. Everything will be all right," she whispered, but, in reality, she had no idea how she would find that wretched cup. She had a feeling that the Christian God would not help her, so she scanned her brain for a spell.

Chapter Three

What is that thing called when just what you needed turns up? Serendipity? The answer to prayers? Morag did not know, but there he sat. The young man sat on a rock, something brought up by the glaciers, in the forest clearing. The lighting took her breath away. It seemed as though Heaven beamed a dose of sunshine into the clearing, while all else remained its usual gloomy grey. Each tiny blade of grass became a truer green, a bright color she had no name for; the opposite of moss. The man's eyes reflected this glorious display, shining a golden color.

Morag feared magic, to some extent. She had not had the best experiences with it. First the cup, and now these cruel, bored sisters. She had no doubt the elf-like human in her midst possessed some other-worldly charm. His cloak, grey wool, was clasped with a pewter oak leaf. Peasants did not possess pewter oak leaves. Yet his bountiful curls, his cherubic expression, and the hint of a smile, made her apprehension go away.

"Greetings, Morag," he spoke.

She approached him, carrying her basket of mushrooms on the crook of her left elbow and keeping the wounded Monty by her right side. He would recover, but he still whimpered. She began to pet him to keep her dog calm.

"Hello, stranger," she replied.

"I heard your call for help. I once helped the king to find his missing sister Catherine, when she had been kidnapped and held prisoner in a cell at Wulfgrim Hall. Princess Beatrice wanted her older sister out of the way so that she could become queen. Her plan did not work out even though Catherine died from her captivity in the cold and damp stone room. Catherine, like you, it seems, loved the outdoors and keeping her underground away from the green of Nature and the light of the sun made her sickly. So I feel as though I've failed, and would like to make it up by aiding you in your quest."

"How do you know my quest, stranger?" a worried Morag asked.

"Somehow I have been born with the power of *seeing* things that others do not. Both a gift and a curse, I suppose, but it would be my pleasure to help you find the Enchanted Cup, Mademoiselle."

"And what is your name, so that I may address you properly?"

"I am called Giles. I confess that once I was an apprentice to Medard, chief sorcerer of Northborough. However, due to my hopelessness at spells, I was dismissed. Fired, really. Still, I learned much from my time in the castle. And I heard of the Enchanted Cup that brought your brother Ranaulf to Caradon Hall. I believe that I may be able to locate it."

Morag realized that meddling in magic usually did not turn out well. Nevertheless, what could she do? Cigfa and Branwen had threatened to kill her dog. She had no choice.

"Then, Giles, please would you help me? I would be indebted to you. Come and have some tea in my cottage."

"Sure, of course, Morag. I will do what I can." They walked together, along with Monty, though the forest, which had become gloomy and dark, as usual. The old ways had served her and her family for generations. She had no reason to convert to the new faith, at least not yet.

CHAPTER FOUR

Morag boiled water for the tea. She made her own blends, In fact, she prided herself on the aromatic and healing teas that she concocted on her own. She dried chamomile flowers for recovery from illness. Rose hips full of health benefits. Mint leaves stopped stomach aches. She used lavender or whatever flower bloomed just to see how it tasted, usually good. She made some blended tea for herself and her guest, setting them down before the simple wooden chairs and table in the main room.

Morag had never been good at small talk, but neither had Giles. So they sat in a companionable silence. Monty thumped his tail on the floor beneath Morag; Giles lost in thought, wondering how he would find the dragon's cup for her. He kept imagining seeing it, in his mind's eye. But waves of thought pushed it further and further away. Would it remain in Northborough, he wondered? In Albion? The silence felt strange. He thought that perhaps he should ask her about her family, but then he remembered that she had none, save Ranaulf.

"And how is Ranaulf doing, mademoiselle?" he asked.

She glared at him and gave him the side-eye. Apparently, he had asked the wrong question. "*Sir* Ranaulf, you mean? The saintly one who left me and our parents alone while he lived in a castle? That one? The one who now is known far and wide for having built the beautiful Church of the Holy Sandal? Surely you know better than I, as I have not seen him since his one visit here."

"Ah, well, I am sorry to hear that," he stuttered. She had shown a flash of anger. He thought perhaps that was his cue to leave. "Now I see the sun setting in the west, and so I will trouble you no further. Thank you so much for your hospitality, Morag." he quickly said, anxious to be on his way.

"I didn't mean to be so harsh. I guess it's just an ongoing open sore I feel from being the sturdy, reliable child, while Ranaulf went on all of his adventures. I have lived in this cottage, not venturing far, my whole life, while he has even traveled across the Narrow Sea! Something I will never do! I have cared for our parents without a thought to myself. Perhaps it is jealousy that I feel toward my brother. But I cannot escape it."

"Do not worry, Morag. I understand your feelings, and I want to help you. Hopefully the fates will show me the location of your cup. Thank you again for the delicious tea and I will see you soon!" He gave Monty a little wave as he left as quickly as he could.

Oh no, thought the girl. *Now I've done it. My big mouth and my hostility toward men. I need to watch that. I wonder if I have scared him off. How much longer do I have until those witches visit me again, this time perhaps really hurting dear Monty?* She feared, taking the last sip of tea as the sun went down, shrouding her and her dog in darkness.

End Of Book I

Book II

Leisure for Rights

Chapter One

King Morvan had been through so much. Ordinanaily, he'd just want to sleep. His travels to the Holy Land, his finding a sandal, being tricked, the journey home, it had taken a lot out of him. Plus, he did not feel as though he rightfully ruled Northborough. After all, it had been Chlodomir who was given the Sandal, given *the actual one that Jesus had worn*, by the unicorn in the monastery. But, silly boy, Chlodomir had gone up the stairs to save someone who did not believe, someone who worked against him. Like the Savior himself, Chlodomir gave up his life for those who neither appreciated nor merited it. But Gondebald feared death. And Chlodo did everything in his power to save him.

Chlodomir would have ruled wisely, reflected Morvan. But perhaps the monk was just *too nice*. Sometimes kings need to use force; sometimes they need to make difficult decisions and compromise their values. Already he felt the weight of his crown upon his head. Another thing to get used to. Granted, it had not been the biggest one he'd seen, but even its delicacy, its intricate etchings, the pearls, sapphires and diamonds within the silver circlet, weighed more than a simple hat. He thought of it as a weight, not only in pounds, but on his soul, to make good decisions for his people. For he loved his people and wanted the best for them.

Morvan thought about his journey to the Holy Land. Was it laziness that made him accept the false sandal for his very valuable sword? Was it laziness that meant that he slept while being robbed? What was wrong with him, and why did he always want to sleep? Sir Ranaulf, one of his advisors, suggested that he read through all of the laws of Northborough in order to get a feel for the legislative and executive situation at hand. "Read through all the laws?" Like, just take a random afternoon and analyze hundreds of parchment papers? Ahhh! The thought burdened him too much.

Morvan wondered for a moment if he had inherited this lack of industry from his father, Mesmin. Everyone loved Mesmin. He naturally attracted fun and friendship. After his alcohol problem, he really sorted out his life. Mesmin's other problem was listening to Beatrice, his wife. Bea had some seriously dangerous ideas, including imprisoning her sister Catherine and poisoning the Knights of the White Hare. Perhaps he resembled his father too much? But the idea of studying a local borough's laws put him to sleep.

Northborough's laws governed the selling of wool, the wages of peasants, the tariffs on foreign trade, mostly with Gaul, and the amount of money owed for causing injury. Rules existed to punish every sort of crime, from theft to poaching in the forest, to murder. Laws governed who repaired the bridges and who paid. And he should read all of this? Morvan did not think so. There were underlings to execute laws. People who actually cared. He was king, and had more important things to do. Perhaps hiring musicians for the court? Planning festivals? Something along those lines, he thought.

Should he seek out the former King, Niall's, assistance? Morvan wondered if Niall even grasped earthly things; he seemed more of an otherworldly presence, the sort who hears angels' voices as he strolls the monastery halls. The king thought of his schooling. Perhaps the years of lessons, boring, boring lessons, were the reason for his not desiring to study up on legalese and pages of minutia. He was never the top student, but that never bothered him. Gondebald tutored him in all things. He learned of magic and spells, herbology, divination, reading runes, and care of creatures. Gondebald hit him when he made mistakes, but he learned soon enough. He had managed the basics. Now he found himself in a royal castle in charge of the everyday lives of humans. Do you see the difference? Hum-ho in every respect. He just could not get into it.

Choosing his crown had been fun, at least. His clothing, warm and elegant, was trimmed with ermine and fox. They wanted him to wear lace but he refused. His under-tunic was made of silk, his stockings as well. Leather shoes kept his feet warm in the stone castle. The design of tapestries interested him; he made a mental note to find out who was in charge of those. And how about a royal ball? That sounds fun! But laws? The daily strife of merchants and peasants? *Pl-ease!* Ranaulf could not have been serious.

Chapter Two

Morvan liked his idea very much. He walked to his mother's rooms. Her suite included a solar, or sitting room, bedroom and bath. She could look out the window upon the fields and forests of Northborough. Finally she lived in a castle of importance! Not that Wulfgrim Hall was not beautiful; of course it was. However, here at Caradon Hall, she had many responsibilities. She lived in the very center of activity! Re-building many of the rooms, especially the turret at the summit, required planning and interior design knowledge. The fire had consumed the tapestries; it burnt the furniture and blackened the stone walls. Beatrice believed that no one but her could restore everything to its former beauty--and more.

So she had been busy with that, as well as decorating her own rooms. Such fun! And now her son had asked her to plan a May Day celebration. No problem! Already she had ordered some pickled fish, bacon and many, many vegetables. The royal hunters would supply game. Farmers will provide the cheeses of many types. Brewers will furnish the ale and vintners the wine.

No party is complete without entertainment, so Bea thought about how she could arrange something new. There usually were lute and harp players, drums, acrobats and jesters. Yet how ordinary. She believed that everyone had tired of these same old, same old entertainers. Bea gazed out her window. There birds flew in circles, looping around, looking for some treat to eat. That's it! She realized that dancers would be the key to her May Day amusement. Dancers who would dress like birds and move gracefully between the revelers. They would carry the pale pastel ribbons from the May Pole while winding around the guests. *Now,* she *thought, where will I find these dancers?*

Chapter Three

Giles liked helping people. He was just that kind of person. Blessed, as he knew, with a supernatural ability to see things other humans could not, he knew that he led a charmed life. Why was he so lonely, then? Walking along the shore, inhaling the seaside scent, he pondered this question. Giles took a seat on a rock. The bottom half, covered in seaweed, swayed underwater as the tide rolled in. He removed his loafers and kicked the soft blueness. He wanted to ask the air, the water, the sun and the moon why no one spoke to him. But he knew. Naturally he knew. For his gift also served as a curse.

Who would speak to a human who also discerned the truth from lies? Who saw right into their hearts, knowing where falsehood replaced honesty? Alas, Giles feared that he would die alone. Perhaps alone except for his four fairies, but what are they compared to the warmth of a human body? How he desired company, if only someone to hold hands with! To hug, to cuddle! Giles felt his burden heavily. He thought of himself as a good and loving person. So why did he live such a lonesome life?

He had tried to envision the Enchanted Cup, he really had. Giles lit a very powerful candle; one made from beeswax, with added essential oils. He entered into a trance-like state, and meditated. *Nothing* at all came to him, but the distressed face of the woman Morag. He knew he could do this! After all, did he not find Princess Catherine? But now he realized something. Perhaps his skills do not work for inanimate objects, only humans. Or perhaps there had been a spell placed upon the cup, preventing him from seeing it. Well, he had one more option, and it had better work.

Giles pulled the little singing bowl from his pocket. Medard had given this parting gift to him, crafted in the East centuries ago. Had he mentioned his fairies? Oh yes, the little ones, sisters, quadruplets. Each one, gold from head to toe. They sported the standard fairy wings. These fairies, however, possessed super-strength, being able to fly long distances. He knew not whether most fairies could do so. But now, Giles used the little mallet to call them from the four directions. Using a stirring motion, he brought forth a deep vibration, like the sound of the universe, like "ohm." He very gently called North and East. They flew in front of him laughing, so happy to be free. Then he did the same, releasing South and West. These two, shining golden in the setting sun, flew and giggled like schoolchildren. He watched them with a bittersweet expression. How happy they were! Why could he not be happy, too, since he had even more freedom than they? Then he put his arm out like a perch for a falcon, and the four fairies came to rest upon it.

"North, East, South and West, I have a serious mission for you. I need to find something, and I cannot 'see' it with my inner vision. So I am asking for your help. Will you help me?"

"Yes! Yes!" each fairy spoke in a teeny, high-pitched voice, eager for their assignments.

"I am certain that you remember the Enchanted Cup? The one made of pewter, centuries ago, with the gruesome visage of a dragon on one side? The cup that sent Ranaulf to Caradon Hall, leaving his poor parents alone and brokenhearted?"

"Yes we do!" they replied in unison, sounding like chipmunks.

"Ranaulf has a sister; her name is Morag. The witches Cigfa and Branwen have been tormenting her, asking her to give them the Cup. For you may remember that Ranaulf once visited his sister and they believe that he gave her the Cup. However, that is not true. She knows not where it landed, and now the witches promise to harm her mangy, lovable dog Monty if she does not give them the cup. Unfortunately, she has no idea where it is; neither do I. Please, would you consider going to your four directions and scouring the Earth, looking for this Enchanted cup for me?"

"Yes! Please send us!" they all cried out enthusiastically, beating their wings like hummingbirds. They looked a little like hummingbirds, actually, thought Giles at this point.

"Well, you have my gratitude. Please go right away. I will miss you. You are my only friends. But I cannot bear to see Monty and Morag suffer, simply for the amusement of Cigfa and Branwen. Just one more thing--remember not to drink even one drop from the Cup if you find it. Thank you all."

They buzzed off like drunken bumblebees. But they were happy, glad to be able to help out. Giles knew that if they could not find the Cup, no one could. Each went in her own direction; they would blanket the Earth. Giles remembered a sermon Brother Bede had given, explaining how the wind was the result of angels' breath. He breathed in each direction, just for good luck, just in case the new religion had something to it.

Chapter Four

The New Order of the Pegasus gathered around their circular table. No one sat at the head; no one at the foot. All were, in a sense, equal. But this meeting had been called because some of the residents of Northborough did not feel as though they received equal treatment under the law. Some had logged complaints that certain merchants had been allowed to cheat their customers. Some had complained that the fares to cross the river favored the wealthy. Others believed that they suffered an unfair tax burden.

All of this happened while King Morvan planned parties. Kings naturally had to rule. Without autocracy, chaos would reign! Everyone understood that peasants had no rights. It went without saying that females had no rights. Imagine! The knights would not have listened to such nonsense. However, when a commission of barons approached them, the knights listened. The barons believed that each man deserved a fair trial. Justice, a fundamental tenet of free people, should be granted. Judges need to be fair and unbiased. They brought this basic demand to the knights.

"Why should this be written into a law? Do you not receive justice now?" asked Sir George.

"Ha ha!" laughed the petitioners. They refused to reply to such a silly question.

"Why should the king grant your demands?" asked Sir Douglas.

"The king is weak! We have no need for him. What has he accomplished in his reign? He needs us to keep the economy growing. Without our cooperation, his tax revenues would dry up and he would be left with nothing. Our enemies to the north and to the east would destroy us. Surely he understands that us barons recruit peasants to till the fields, to provide food, to work as soldiers. We do not want the king to use his authority to unfairly accuse us, imprison us, take away our possessions, show up with armed forces at our castle. The king does not have the authority to do whatever he pleases. We see the end of absolute monarchy! No king should wield arbitrary power. Our land needs laws to restrict him."

"If we gave in to your demands, who is to say that you will not ask for more and more rights? Today you want guarantees of the rights to possessions, against unfair imprisonment, against political targeting. What will you demand tomorrow if we give in? The right to vote, ha ha?" laughed Sir Douglas.

"Nay, you do not have to worry about such nonsense. Surely the monarchy exists to keep order and the law. What would happen if even barons voted! We are just asking for the right to a fair trial, the right to justice. Could you even imagine if peasants ever voted? It would be the end of society as we know it!"

Here Sir Ranaulf had to intervene. "Fellow knights and honored barons, you do the villein injustice by saying that they are any different from you. I was born a peasant. Only through the magic in the Enchanted Cup do I stand here in this room before you, attired in luxurious clothing, drinking fine wine. And, knowing my family, I can tell you that the peasants are no different from the wealthy and titled. They love their children. They work hard for what little they have. They only ask to be treated fairly, enough to eat, and perhaps, someday, an education. How is it that only the moneyed classes can afford tutors?"

The room became silenced with the shock of Sir Ranaulf's words. What revolutionary thoughts had he uttered? Education for the poor? He had to be joking.

"Let us stick to the issue at hand. We shall bring your petitions to the king. You are dismissed," said Sir George, anxious to end the meeting.

"Thank you, knights of the New Order of the Pegasus, for listening," replied the barons, as they left. But they were not finished.

Chapter Five

Beatrice sincerely enjoyed her new role. While some queen mothers may simply act as figureheads, Bea loved to get involved with the social obligations of her son. She knew exactly how to plan events. She could do it for a living, if she were not royalty, and royals do not work for a living; that is what peasants do. But here at Caradon Hall, after all of the refurbishings, it looked even nicer than before. Perhaps even nicer than Wulfgrim Hall. Naturally, because it had been decorated by her herself. And Bea had good taste, if she did not say so herself.

    Now she became enmeshed in the party planning. Most of it had already been done. She had seen to the food, drink, appetizers, tablecloths, flowers, silverware and decorations. She had hired minstrels and engaged the palace fool. The one thing missing was a dancer or dancers for entertainment, and today was audition day.

    With a drummer accompaniment, she called out, "Five, six, se-ven eight!" as one after the other they performed for her. A dull young girl from the church tried out, but her dancing was uninspired. "No, no, no!" A troupe of male dancers possessed athleticism, able to stand on their hands and do flips, for example, but Bea was bored. She had seen it all before. "Don't call us; we'll call you," she chanted, somewhat nastily. She was quickly losing patience. Perhaps she should call it a day and try again tomorrow. No one was quite right. But then a little face peered out from the curtain, and she figured one more awful audition could not hurt.

"Next!" she brightly exclaimed, and a very young girl with a very sweet face stood before her. The girl's nose turned up like the slope of a mountain. Her eyes sparkled a bright blue like forget-me-nots, and her hair was a darker brown. This acorn-colored hair moved like a curtain all around her body; she hastily pulled it up, tying it into a top-knot as she stood before the queen mother.

"Five, six, se-ven, eight!" Bea clapped along to the drum. What she saw took her breath away. The girl danced like an angel; like the wind. Her movements were as fluid as water; as effortless as a stag's. She bent all the way backward--what core strength! She twisted her body left and right, her long hair flowing alongside. She moved like an animal; quick at one moment, then slowing down. Her hair fell out of its bun, cascading and moving with her body as she leapt, defying the forces which normally hold mortals down. Bea stood mesmerized by this creature who danced this well even without music.

"What is your name?" Bea demanded.

"My name is Ophelia, my lady."

"Your dance intrigues me. Everyone else bored me. You're hired. Be here tomorrow at eight in the morning for practice with the musicians. Do not be late. That is all." And so it began.

Chapter Six

Tiny East had flown for thousands of miles. Exhausted, she fell into a heap onto Giles' lap. Giles sat in his cottage, surprised by her arrival. He startled. "Do not worry; it's only me!" she exclaimed in her tinny voice. Giles relaxed and fell back into the pillow next to him. He set her down upon the pillow as he rose to get her some water. After sipping it greedily, she gave him her report.

"Giles, I have done as you asked. I flew through the middle east and Jerusalem, through the Byzantine Empire; through the Novgorod Republic and the Rus. I flew through Serbia, Croatia and Ukraine. I searched Poland, Hungary, Romania and Greece. I saw Armenia, the Czech lands and finally all the way as far as the land went, to Imperial China. Honestly, Giles, I could not see the cup. In all of those lands, I noticed many magical things; a magical carpet and lamp, for example, in Persia. I witnessed a menorah that burned for eight days, despite having only enough oil for one. I witnessed a tomb where a man who had been dead, walked out alive. But, unfortunately, I did not see the Enchanted Cup anywhere. I am sorry to disappoint you."

Just then another tiny creature flew through the window of the humble cottage. Little South had flown thousands of miles, just like East had. She landed on Giles' chair, exhausted.

"Let me get you a little water to drink," he said.

"Sure, I would love that, but do you have any nectar?"

Giles had to think about that. He did not, actually, but he mixed some water and honey and heated it, making a sweet drink for her. She drank and felt much better.

"Thank you, seer!"

"You're welcome. Are you all right?"

"Yes, I feel better now. I have flown south to warmer climates. I flew to the land of the Aztecs and Mayas, where they have made a calendar. I witnessed llamas who make the warmest wool. I saw a forest so dense, the floor was invisible though the leaves. I viewed a desert so large that it took me hours to fly over it. I saw humans of all different skin colors, a rainbow of diversity. They practiced magic there; Santeria and Voodoo, but I searched and searched but could not spy the Enchanted Cup. I am sorry that I failed."

"You have *not* failed, South. You tried your best, and that is what matters. Thank you so much for your journey. Now, rest." And she did, falling asleep immediately. As soon as South lay down, another golden fairy flew in through the window. This time, North fluttered into his lap, collapsing in a heap, a gorgeous heap, as fairies are iridescent and reflect the sun. This evening, she reflected the colors of the setting sun, rose pink, royal purple and cobalt blue all mixed with the glittering gold of her skin and wings.

"I'm back!" she happily announced, smiling through the pain and exhaustion. "I have visited lands where ice covers all; where the breath is visible; where pastel light shows illuminate the sky at night. The lights look like waving walls of color, like nothing I have seen. I viewed lands never civilized by the Romans, where people live in darkness and the Druids still control everything. Magic lives there, as the sorcerers make daytime turn to night; sunshine into rain, safety into danger, and snow out of nothing at all. You know our own Gondebald, Medard, Mesmin and Lughar. Here is where their magic was born. There I witnessed the quest for the Philosopher's Stone, the Elixir of Life, and heard many spells cast by witches, but, I am sorry to relate, no Enchanted Cup anywhere. I even looked in ice-filled caverns, fjords and mountains, to no avail. I was so cold the whole time! I am glad to be back but very sorry for having failed in my mission."

Giles held her in his hands, hoping to warm her little body. "Do not worry, North. I know that you flew for thousands of miles and searched deeply for the Cup. The people of the North still live in fear of the ancient faith, but one day I see the new one, the one of Christ, surpassing it altogether. In the meantime, just rest and recover from this long trip."

As he spoke his comforting words, North fell asleep. He placed her on his bed, and covered her gently, alongside East and South. Giles felt a weight upon him. His only hope to help Morag lay in the fairy West. Why had she not arrived as yet? He pondered these thoughts as he fell asleep as well.

End of Book II

Book III

A Stranger for a Princess

Chapter One

The small community of Northborough very rarely saw visitors from outside of Albion. Albion was an island, so people had to travel by both land and sea to arrive there. Mikolaj certainly stood out from the average Northborough resident. For one thing, he was pale as the wool of sheep. In contrast, his long hair matched the color of a starless night. Mikolaj's hair fell in many skinny braids down his back and along his face, intertwined with strips of leather. His thinness made his cheekbones stand out; was it lack of nutrition on his long trip? He rode a standard horse, not magnificent but not scruffy, either. The mount was spotted, black with white, quite appealing. His bearing, however, was regal; as he held his head high; his gaze ahead, and his back straight.

The stranger's eyes were warm and brown, like freshly-baked bread. Yet they held a sadness, and they were lined with murky khol. Green flecks spotted the iris. His black tunic was studded with silver. The people wondered about him, who he was, why he had come to their town. He approached Caradon Hall, seeming to understand that there resided the seat of government. Mikolaj turned and stood, facing the citizens.

"Hail, residents of Northborough. I have heard much about your land. The story has traveled all the way to Poland, the land I grew up in. I have traveled through the Holy Roman Empire; through Gaul. I have tried to explain my new theory, but no one has listened. I have been forced to flee every town I have entered. I was hoping to find an open mind and shelter here in your magical kingdom. I also wanted to pray and attend Mass at the Church of the Holy Sandal, if you will allow it."

The people stood in wonder. They whispered among themselves, "What is his new theory and why is it so dangerous that every town in northern Europe has expelled him? He assuredly dresses very strangely. He is probably up to no good. Perhaps he is a spy!"

"Yes, probably a spy! Look at how he dresses in black!"

"Or maybe a sorcerer!"

"The last thing we need--foreigners! Everything has been going well and now *he* shows up. Listen to his voice; it is strange; tinged with an accent!"

Just then someone from the castle noticed the commotion. Godfrey the porter opened the door to see what was happening. He was taken aback upon seeing the stranger, so tall, thin, pale, and clad entirely in black. Yet, he opened the great door.

"Sir, what business have you here? We are a peaceful community."

"Good man, I am here as a humble supplicant. I would like to present my theory on science and the universe to the king. Please may I be admitted?" The porter looked Mikolaj up and down. No, he did not look like a scientist. He more resembled a warrior, a goth.

"And why should I believe you? You look like an unsavory character."

"Please do not judge me based upon my appearance. Inside of my head, ideas circle like carrion birds. I need to draw pictures, to write them down. Using mathematics, I study the stars, eclipses and the sun." Here there was a gasp among the people. Now they KNEW that he *must* be a sorcerer.

Mikolj continued, "I have studied at two renowned universities. I have served as a church canon, collecting rents, overseeing the finances, the bakery and the brewery. You are correct to believe that my Anglo-Saxon English is not perfect. However, beside my native tongue, I also speak German, Frankish,

Latin and Italian. None of them come perfectly from my mouth, alas, but I genuinely would like to speak to your king, if you will please grant me an audience."

Godfrey did not know what to say. This situation had never come up before. Luckily, however, Beatrice came to the door to see what was happening on that lovely April morning.

Chapter Two

Bea had remained lovely throughout her life. Never having to work or wash a dish, her hands still soft, never weeding or reaping the fields, her skin never wrinkled. She took advantage of Mesmin's skills, asking him to provide her with balms and creams to keep her young. She'd never fallen off a horse, knock on wood. She still took Mesmin's breath away; he still loved her and worshipped her like a goddess.

She had heard the commotion outside of the castle and walked down to the front door from her solar. The porter had opened it and stood outside. She lifted her eyes to a stranger, but, oh, what a stranger! Not handsome, as his ears, eyes and nose were all far too big. But arresting, mesmerizing, gripping and what a presence! He resembled no one she had ever met. Perhaps because she had never met anyone from Poland before; no one in Northborough had. He had come so far to see the king! He was after money, no doubt. She could care less. All she wanted to do was spend time with him. She wanted to learn all she could about this interesting stranger and his theory.

To the porter, she said, "Do not worry; I will vouch for him. Come with me. What did you say your name was?"

"My lady, my name is Miklolaj and I am from Poland," he replied with an accent.

Beatrice thought that he had the cutest accent she had ever heard. She could listen to that accent all day. "Please, this way. I would like to hear your story, to see if the king would be interested in what you have to say."

The people gasped. What was going on? The queen mother, who never made an appearance outside of the castle, had come out and welcomed this potentially dangerous migrant inside? Where her son, the king, resided? They did not understand and began to murmur. Just then, a delegation of barons appeared. They dressed in thick and luxurious materials, their higher class apparent to all. They rode fine, well-fed horses, ones that had shiny coats and bright eyes. Their saddles were crafted from good, tanned leather. The crowd grew silent.

Godfrey still stood at the door. What an exhausting morning! Usually his job was quite cushy. Visitors were rare. Now what was he to do? "What is your business here today, good men?" he asked them.

"We were here before. We have not yet heard back from the king."

At that, from behind trees everywhere emerged armed men. They marched slowly and steadily to the gathering in front of Caradon Hall.

The barons simply waited.

"Let me get the king," stammered the porter, clearly shaken.

Chapter Three

Morvan had better things to do than to give away the rights of the monarchy. After all, it had progressed thus for centuries. The royals were the only ones who had blue blood, who knew instinctively how to rule. For all of history, the royal families in every country made and enforced the law. They were one in the same.

These barons, asking for "justice," for "fair trials," should be ashamed of themselves. They knew better! They, at least for the most part, were literate and understood the way of things.

The king opened the great door at the front of the castle. He would have cursed if he were that kind of person, but having been raised gently, did not use coarse words like a commoner. He merely said them in his mind. Before him stood the delegation of barons who had spoken to the New Order of the Pegasus. He had told the knights where the barons could put their ideas! He had better uses of his time. Didn't they know that after the fire, much of Caradon Hall needed redecorating? Merchants from around the world brought him their wares, lamps, tapestries, paintings. Besides, his mother was planning the biggest fete ever to grace the kingdom--a massive May Day party and ceremony--and he wanted to help. He had no time for this nonsense about granting rights to the lower class!

As he stepped out, hundreds of men raised their weapons. There would be a massacre if he did not acquiesce. Fine. *Have your little trials by jury*, he thought. It will never change the course of history. Kings still will have absolute rights to do as they please.

"Gentlemen, what brings you here this sunny spring day?" he asked.

"We thought that we had a productive talk with the New Order of the Pegasus, that they would bring our petitions to you. But we have heard nothing, and we grow restless." At that, one of the barons handed him a scroll of parchment. Written upon it were their demands.

No free man shall be seized or imprisoned, or stripped of his rights or possessions, or outlawed or exiled, or deprived of his standing in any other way, nor will we proceed with force against him, or send others to do so, except by the lawful judgement of his equals or by the law of the land. To no one will we sell, to no one deny or delay right or justice.

The king tossed back his head and laughed heartily. "Ha ha! Surely you jest?"

"No, certainly we don't. The time has come for liberty and justice. These are the ideas that are sweeping the continent. All free men should have the right to a fair trial, the right to their possessions. A man should be tried by a jury of his peers. Naturally we are not speaking about women or slaves here. With liberty, men will work harder! They will become motivated to prosper! The merchant class is growing and will become the foundation of our prosperity.

The people should not be taxed wantonly. Just because you want to have a party, you should not increase taxes!" The people were shocked. What kind of words were these? They had never heard anything like it. They agreed wholeheartedly, but who spoke to a king thus?

"We hereby rescind our oath of allegiance to you, King Morvan."

The king, shocked, exclaimed, "What have you just said? You cannot do that! I am the king! *Je suis le roy! Le etat, c'est moi*, as they say, ha ha. Next thing you know, you will be asking for the vote!" He felt heated under his ermine.

Here, again, the people cried out. The vote? What on earth is a *vote*? They had no idea, but were beginning to really like what the barons demanded. "The VOTE! The VOTE!" They chanted. But now the king began to worry. He was clearly outnumbered. If he agreed to the barons' demands, maybe he could just "forget" about having signed the document. Clearly, as leader, he had to do *something*. Oh, the heaviness of wearing a crown!

The barons countered, "Let's not get ahead of ourselves here. No one is calling for democracy or that one-man-one-vote nonsense. Surely the peasants have no idea what their own best interest is. That is why we represent them. But if you do not sign our document, King Morvan, we will no longer pay our tribute to you. Our peasants will no longer fight for you. So decide, and stop wasting our time. We become restless. They raised their weapons again. They took a step forward.

Morvan looked at Ranaulf, who naturally stood beside him. Ranaulf nodded his head, and the lead baron walked up to His Majesty, offering the document of liberty along with a feathered quill. Morvan looked down to hide his tears as he signed. Later, the king's clerks made copies for distribution to the churches in Northborough, sealed with the royal seal. And so a quiet revolution for the rights of man began, and this was the moment. Many more moments, many more struggles, were needed before a commorner, whatever his or her skin color, gender, disability or other distinction, could claim the same legal status as a titled person or royalty, but here witnessed many in Northborough, a truly magical moment.

Chapter Four

Beatrice felt her knees and became weak. She had never felt this way before. She kept wanting to laugh out loud! To jump and spin around like a swallow! Seeing the stranger, the darkly-clad Mikolaj, made her think inappropriate thoughts. What was she doing; she, a long-married woman, in a very happy marriage, becoming besotted with a foreigner who spoke English with an accent? Who dressed so strangely, who arrived as a supplicant? What was wrong with her?

Yet this magnetic attraction she felt forced her to speak to him.

"Dear sir, please follow me. I will bring you to the king," she said, gently guiding his arm. She moved her head in the direction of her stableman, who understood her desire for him to take care of Mikolaj's horse.

They walked to Morvan's chamber and knocked. "It's me," she said, and the porter opened the door. He entered and she left, letting them talk. Unknown to her, Mesmin had been watching everything. Through magic, he could see anything he wanted to. And, unfortunately, he had noticed how his beautiful wife reacted to the stranger. He may have been old, he may have lacked comeliness, but he did not lack brains. Poor Mesmin, of the good heart, let his head fall upon his lap. He had always thought that this moment would come. That his stunning wife would find someone else. And now, he thought, it had happened.

I can just use magic to make her hate him, he reasoned. No doubt that was true. But did he want to force his wife to love him, if she did not? Have all of their years together been simply a sham? "UUUUUUGGGGGHHHH!" He screamed, "NO, NO, NO! Noooooooooo!" Mesmin collapsed into crying. His head banged down upon the table; he sobbed. He had never cried his whole adult life. Life was unfair, he thought, and felt sadder than he could remember. He felt as though his heart had literally broken into pieces. The pain was unbearable. They call it unrequited love. He wished that he did not love Bea as much as he did. If only, he thought, he had not just watched this scene, as he knew what would happen next.

Mesmin called to his servant. "Get me a cup of wine, lad," he mumbled between sobs. The only thing he knew to salve the pain was the fruit of the vine. It had been years, but the first taste reawakened the desire of his heart. Here, he believed, he would find the only lover who loved him back, le vin. Le vin would keep him company when his wife deserted him.

End of Book III

Book IV

A Fairy for a Cup

Chapter One

The king sat behind his desk and gestured for his guest to have a seat. "May I get you some wine, some bread or cheese?"

"I am a knight of the Twin Eagles," said Mikolaj, so you may call me 'Sir.' Look, here is my crest upon my tunic. The red eagles face each other on a red field. Do not worry, the Pope has approved us. I am no sorcerer, your majesty. I am simply an academic, but I am quite famished from my journey, so, yes, let us have a meal together."

Morvan motioned to a servant, who brought a tray of food. The two men ate in silence for a while. Then the king asked, "My guest, what brings you to Northborough?"

Mikolaj responded, "King Morvan, thank you so much for this audience. I have travelled across Europe looking for a sponsor. I spoke to the kings of Poland, the Holy Roman Empire, Gaul and now you. No one has agreed. I am hoping that you are more progressive and forward-thinking than the others."

"And what is your theory, Sir?"

"You see, my calculations have proven that the Earth is not actually sitting in the center of the Universe. The Sun, rather, lies in the very center."

Morvan gasped. So did the servants in the room. They smelled the scent of evil. Surely this was a bad man with bad magic. Even Morvan, not the most religious person in the world, knew that the Bible said that the Earth lived at the center of the Universe.

"Ha, ha," he said. "You are joking, right? Anyone can look up into the sky and watch as the sun revolves around our planet. It is plain as day, pardon the pun! But one would have to be simple to believe otherwise. Do all men's eyes lie?"

Mikolaj had heard this objection before. He replied, "Your majesty, I agree with you that it looks as though the sun revolves around the earth. That is how it seems to me, as well. However, my mathematical calculations prove that it is otherwise."

The men took some bites of the bread and cheese, washed down by the goblets of wine. Then the king responded, "Mikolaj, you seem like a decent chap. Much as I would like to sponsor you, I feel as though I might be deposed by my people for feeble-mindedness! Who would possibly believe such nonsense! Even for fun, I could not do it. In fact, while I have enjoyed getting to know you, I think you should leave immediately."

Bea nearly choked. She held in a cough. She had been hiding behind a curtain and heard the whole conversation. This could not be happening--not when she finally found someone who made her heart jump and made her feet want to dance. She backed away, walked around the hallway and then knocked at the door.

"Yes?" asked Morvan.

"It's only me, your mum!" she sweetly responded.

"Come in, then, woman. We are at men's affairs right now. What is it that you need? Do you have a question about the party that cannot wait? Decorations?, perhaps?"

"No, I just...I just..." Here she paused as she was unable to speak. "Morvan, do I have your permission to speak to our guest in private?"

"Naturally, Mother. He may be able to fill you in on some recipes from abroad. We get so few visitors here, after all. That is fine with me. You both are dismissed."

Chapter Two

Beatrice led the stranger to her solar. They sat, facing each other, over the light of a candle placed in the center of a table. The soft glow of candlelight brought their faces closer. As Bea looked into Mikolaj's eyes, she hoped that he felt the same way as she did. She asked him, "now, what will you do as my son has rejected you?"

"I have one more option," he replied. "I have studied in Italy and they are more open-minded than other nations. There seem to grow the stirrings of a new philosophy. I need to go back and show them my theories and my proofs. If they do not believe me, no one will. They have begun to question religion in place of humanism. They understand that some of the words in the Bible are there only for our education, not necessarily to be understood literally. The people of Greece and Italy are bringing back the books and discoveries of the ancients. This re-birth of classical culture has loosened the ties to the universal Church, allowing free thinking.

"My ideas are not at all contrary to the teachings of the Catholic Church. I firmly believe in both science and God. After all, it was God who gave us this Earth and the physical, biological and chemical laws to which all of nature must obey. My mathematical computations have merely shown me more of His beautiful creation, more of His unfathomable plan. How can it matter if the Earth revolves around the Sun or the other way around? Does that change revelation? Is Jesus not still God's only and divine Son? I get so frustrated sometimes with the closed minds of these religious and royal leaders!"

Beatrice thought about what the visitor said. She still stuck with the old Druidic religion, so these debates did not concern her. But she could feel the pain in Mikolaj's voice. He seemed so sincere; so genuine. The leaders always got their way, and it was not fair. She wanted to give him a chance.

"Look at me, Sir Mikolaj." She took her first two fingers and gently lifted up his fallen chin. "I will help you with money for your voyage--as long as I may accompany you. I will be able to help you to see kings who otherwise would not grant you an audience. We would need to travel through Gaul, and perhaps visit Spain along the way. What do you say?"

Mikolaj sat stunned into silence. Many terrible thoughts ran through his mind. "What about your husband, lady? Surely he would disapprove of such a trip." But he only said this as he knew her heart. Obviously she was in love with him, and he would have to go along with this charade if his ideas would see the light of day.

Beatrice waited before responding. *Of course* Mesmin would be upset. She recognized his great powers, accepting that he could ruin the journey for them. Mesmin could make their horses become lame, or cause her and Mikolaj to suffer illness. He could put warding spells around the castles of the other countries, barring them entrance. But Bea didn't care. No one was going to destroy her happiness. If Mikolaj does not receive his funding or his recognition, who cares? She still would be with him. And, right now, that was *all* she wanted in the whole world.

"Don't worry about him," she retorted. "Leave that to me. Just prepare yourself for our journey. I heard that you wanted to see our famous Church of the Holy Sandal, so we will leave tomorrow after Mass."

In the meantime, she schemed a plan to make him hers. Why would a handsome young knight be interested in the mother of the king, anyway? She knew her time of loveliness had passed. It hurt, but all of the creams and salves in Northborough could not eliminate every wrinkle and crow's foot. Her once-thick red hair had thinned. She was not stupid, but she had some magical powers of her own. Tonight she planned to look up the spell on the most-worn page in her book, the one for a Love Potion. There were more of these than others, so she needed to read through the various options, seeing which ingredients she had. She recalled long ago, how she had made such a potion for Mesmin. Her plan to have her son sit on the throne of Northborough had worked. How strange time is, she thought. Now she is making a similar potion for a stranger.

Chapter Three

Bea hummed to herself. She feared the outcome of her spell, but why not give it a try? The worst that could happen would be that it failed. She gathered together all of the ingredients, and prepared a fire under her mini-cauldron. The cauldron, composed of iron, sat upon a little fire. She had picked the plants at midnight, as prescribed. Some of the ingredients potentially could be dangerous, even deadly. But, following the recipe, she carefully mixed them and cooked them. She combined mandrake, henbane, verbena, honey and rose water. Her love potion, complete, cooled in her room.

Meanwhile, just to make sure, she had a gift for Mikolaj. She had a collection of ancient artifacts, this one known for love. It was a green molded silver miniature statue of a woman, with crystal stones for the eyes, on a leather cord. The amulet's name was Freya, and she hoped it would help in her cause.

As dawn blossomed, she prepared her bag of clothes for the journey. She made sure to pack clothes for warm as well as cold weather, and her potions and book of magic spells. She tucked the amulet and love potion within the clothing for protection.

After washing and dressing in her most beautiful but travel-worthy gown, she went to see if Mikolaj was ready. Her plan, leaving so early, was for Mesmin not to notice. She walked by his room and heard sonorous snores. *Check*, she said to herself, *he will not know until she is gone.*

"Come, Sir Mikolaj," she said to him, after knocking softly on his door. "Mass is about to begin." Everyone knew the Mass schedule, whether attending or not, as it was really the only social event that everyone was invited to. At that point, she realized that she would miss the palace May Day ball. At that point, she realized that she didn't care. Bea was just too excited to begin her journey south with the intriguing stranger. She made a mental note to find someone to take over the planning and preparations for the ball.

Chapter Four

Mikolaj woke up with a start. Someone was knocking at his door. He looked around. Never had he slept in so sumptuous a bed! The sheets were soft, made of lamb's wool. A canopy floated above him; everything a muted off-white color like the color of pearls. Pillows made of lace surrounded his face. On the nightstand stood a vase full of lilies as well as a bowl to wash his face with. The tapestries lining the stone walls of the castle were elegant and detailed, showing scenes of the daily lives of the peasants. Here a woman washed clothes at the river; here a man dyed wool. A shepherd, a farmer, a merchant all labored upon those walls. The tapestries carried golden threads throughout. These threads of gold reflected the sunlight which beamed into his chamber. He got up slowly, wondering what the pounding was all about.

Before answering, he splashed his face with water, drying it hastily with the cream-colored towel. "Yes?" he inquired.

"It's me," Bea said, as if they were lifelong friends. "Time to leave for Mass, or we will be late!"

"Oh, yes, I will be right there." Tumbled-looking as he was, he opened the door. Bea caught her breath. His long braids stood up all around his head. He looked quite adorable tousled. He stood there in a nightshirt.

"You will need to put on some nicer clothes," she said, blushing.

"Of course, I will only be a minute," Mikolaj replied, closing the door on the queen mother, but not really knowing what else he could have done. It would have been inappropriate to invite her inside. It was customary to fast before Mass, as the Host was the only thing that should be in one's mouth or stomach as you receive communion. So neither offered food nor drink to the other, as awkward as that seemed. He dressed in his traveling wardrobe and opened the door.

Bea looked at his messy appearance and approved. While most Northborough residents put on their Sunday finest to go to church, she understood that Mikolaj had not packed much. He traveled upon a horse and that was all he could bring. Yet, he smelled fresh and clean from washing, and she inhaled it, enjoying this scent. At the same time she admonished herself for these feelings. Why could she not feel the same way for Mesmin? He was a good man, a truly good man, who was in love with her. She inwardly berated herself for these feelings that entered her heart but she could not control.

Chapter Five

They mounted their horses and rode to the church. The brand-new Church of the Holy Sandal had been built with loving kindness by the local people, who had donated time and materials for its construction. Surely, after the great fire in Caradon Hall, there was sacred dust in the ground. Upon this hallowed ground, the church was built. Not tall, like Notre Dame in Paris, but stocky and solid-looking, the stone building nevertheless featured deeply colored stained glass windows. The windows, made by local artisans, depicted the finding and destruction of the Holy Sandals.

From Gondebald's shocking discovery of a Sandal in his turret-room, to Clodomir's being given its mate by the unicorn, from Morvan's dangerous journey to the Holy Land, to his being deceived by a merchant of relics, to the presentation to the sorcerer of the two sandals, these were crafted by artists in molten glass. Windows showed the old mage taking the Sandal from Chlodomir and then igniting his own room. The last scene depicts the castle in flames. The story went around the church walls.

Inside, detailed paintings told the story of the Stations of the Cross. A bowl for baptisms stood carved from white marble streaked with golden veins. The altar had been carved from wood with symbols of the Alpha and the Omega. On the left side of the altar, a beautiful statue of Our Lady wearing a blue gown, her hands folded in prayer and her head gently bent downward in humility. On the right side of the altar, Saint Joseph, in a maroon garment, stood holding a staff of lilies.

Behind the altar, the resurrected Jesus stood solemnly, with one hand pointing to his Sacred Heart, and the other in a sign of blessing. The artist brought forth a look of love and longing in His eyes. To gaze into these eyes, the parishioner saw how much he or she was beloved by God. It felt so warm and comforting. The pews were hewn from local oak trees. Nothing fancy, just sturdy and relatively comfortable. Women of the Altar Society had brought vases full of cut wildflowers.

They sat in front, as royalty and knights ought. The common folk in pews behind tried to whisper softly about the incredible sight before them. The king's mother and a foreigner in the parish! It was difficult concentrating with these two in front, Bea looking majestic in a feathered white gown, knotted with pearls, and the stranger all in black wool and leather. "She looks like a bride! How scandalous!"

Mesmin did not attend church services, but saw everything through his abilities. If his heart could break into even more pieces, it deteriorated at that moment. He felt a physical pain, as if a glass heart sent shards into his chest cavity. Then he felt it melting, moulding, turning into slime and churning within himself. "Oh, stop, please stop this!" he cried out. But no one heard.

In the church, the choir's voices lifted the parishioners' mood. This was the one time all week they experienced the most exalted of European culture. Day by day they labored in the fields, making beer, dying or sewing fabric, caring for children or tending to animals. Sundays their souls and minds rose above these routine chores.

Brother Bede's homily discussed the Sermon on the Mount. The Mass, spoken in Latin, while beautiful, was incomprehensible to most parishioners. However, they loved hearing Brother Bede reflect upon the Word of God in English. Jesus' words here seemed to console them, telling them that though they may face drudgery on this earth, they will be rewarded in Heaven. They resolved to keep doing the right thing; to fulfill their duties and to worship and respect their Lord.

Even when their neighbor stole their food; when they were falsely accused, when they felt as if no one were lower in wealth or position than they, when they were teased for being Christian, they needed to bear these crosses happily, for Heaven waited with open arms. Heaven looked only at their hearts, not their money, their status, how richly they were attired, nor whether or not they owned land. In this way, their faith was a great leveler. In this way, they felt a little snug and warm inside. Someday it will all be worth it.

Chapter Six

After genuflecting as they left the Church of the Holy Sandal, Mikolaj and Beatrice waited to speak to Brother Bede. He made the sign of the cross upon each of them, one at a time. He sprinkled holy water upon their cloaks. Mikolaj explained to Bede his heliocentric theory. He told him that he is not fully sure that it is correct, but nearly so.

In his mind, Brother Bede is feeling very afraid. His "evil" sensors are up; his round body is sweating. He must get this scoundrel out of Northborough. So he says to Mikolaj, "Sir, go thou in peace. You have my blessing." Inside, he is thinking, *the sooner this stranger leaves our land, the better.*

As they walked to where the horses were tethered, a strange sight greeted them. Bea gasped as she saw her mount, with his luxurious saddle and blanket, leaning forward. As she approached, she noticed the poor horse's front legs were a foot shorter than his back legs. The look on his face was one of sadness and desperation. Then Mikolaj looked upon the shocked face of his own horse, the one who had faithfully and dutifully taken him across Europe. The horse looked down upon him from legs a foot longer in front than in back. There was nothing they could do; the horses no longer were rideable.

Beatrice and Mikolaj asked Brother Bede if there were any spare horses belonging to the church, and there was only his own old, slow, sway-backed mare. She would have to do. Bea told Mikolaj to wait there while she rode to the castle. Brother Bede took this opportunity to give the visitor a tour of the new church and grounds. He also showed him his own new and quite modern little apartment, although it was furnished, like Clothilde's, with only a bed and crucifix, a chest of drawers and a bowl of water. Still, its window looked out upon the forest, and Bede loved it. He could sit inside his room, read The Bible or his book of devotions, and gaze upon the beauty of God's creation. What more could anyone ask?

The cleric then showed Mikolaj the brewery in the basement, where the mead and beer were fermented. they shared a cup of fellowship. Mikolaj explained his plan, to head south to where the Renaissance was beginning, in Milan, to try to find a sponsor for his radical new idea. Bede said that he hoped this wish would come true, and inwardly apologized for his sin of lying. No, thought Bede, *I actually don't hope that anyone will sponsor your heretical ideas, but good luck, nevertheless.* This Mikolaj fellow wasn't all bad, and seemed better and better with each glass of spirits.

Finally, as darkness neared, Beatrice arrived riding a comely horse with one trailing behind it. In the morning they would transfer the saddles, blankets and bridles. their poor horses had laid down upon the ground, and Bea wondered if they would even live. It was not like her husband to treat animals this way, but who else could have done it? She felt very uneasy. Is Mesmin there with them or just watching through magic? Either way, guilt covered her like a shroud. For she was guilty, and she knew it. But there was no going back now. They would set out in the morning for Italy. She knew the Christians said, "Go with God," or "Godspeed." She turned over in the straw cot Brother Bede had provided for the mother of the king. Yet she had nothing to say.

She greeted a grey sky the next morning, heavy with rain. Alas, rain comes and goes, but the timing was unfortunate. She had brought heavy cloaks for herself and Mikolaj. In the back of her mind, she wondered if Mesmin was behind this, too. Are his powers that deep? Surely Gondebald could summon the weather, but she could only hope that this spring shower had been called by Mother Nature rather than by him. Oh well, as they say, a journey of a thousand miles begins with a single step. It is that first step which is the hardest.

End of Book IV

Book V

A Fairy for a Cup

Chapter One

Just when Giles thought that poor West had perished, the tiny fairy flew into his window and toward him, collapsing into his arms. He gently fed her honey-water through a soaked rag. Then she slept. All he could do was hope that she would awaken. He let her sleep and recuperate. He wondered if a song would help, so he gently sang to her.

My fairy, not the least,

My fairy, of the west,

My fairy, the color of cheddar cheese,

My fairy, you're the best.

Well, he had made it up on the spot. He never said he was a musician or singer, just a seer. He told himself that obviously gold was not the same color as the bright orange of their good Albion cheese, but close enough. The sun set and he got up for some dinner. Then, as morning dawned, little West began to stir.

First things first, and they shared some food. Then, she was ready to talk. Breaking bread and chewing hungrily, he asked her what she had seen.

But West could barely speak. She faded away, rather than strengthening. "I saw…" she murmured. "I saw…"

"What did you see?" he asked her, worried that he would never know. He immediately upbraided himself silently for this thought.

"I saw…the cup."

"The cup! Where, West, did you see the cup?"

"A…mer… i…ca." West whispered, collapsed, and breathed her last breath.

Chapter Two

Giles hugged the little fairy to his chest. *Oh no*, he thought. *Oh, this poor thing. This poor little angel has just given her life for the sake of that evil dragon's cup and those scheming sisters. It's just not fair at all. Not at all.* A tear wandered down his cheek and fell upon the body of the sweet golden fairy. *Now what?* He wondered.

"I suppose I should bring her to Brother Bede," he said to himself. He got up and put a cloak on. He placed her inside a pocket. He really did not know what to do, but Brother Bede would know. He walked to the Church of the Holy Sandal, where he saw Goslar gathering up a bucket of dirt from around the building. He was too upset to think twice about it, other than how strange that seemed to him.

"Is anyone home?" he asked.

Brother Bede came hurrying upstairs to see what was the matter. He loved helping people. After all, that is why he went into this profession, as well as having felt a "calling" to serve the Lord. Sometimes being a religious brother could be lonely. there were hours and hours when he spoke to no one; but became lost in prayer or adoration of the Blessed Sacrament. He visited his parishioners as often as possible, and brought alms to the poor. Bede loved cooking and hosted dinner parties and being invited to dinner. He brewed his ale and mead; he fermented grapes for wine, which were, naturally, a necessary part of the Mass. But there were times when he felt alone, having chosen a profession without the possibility of marriage and children.

Brother Bede sometimes wondered if anyone loved him. There were, he understood, different kinds of love. There was the perfect love that God had for him and all His creatures. There was the love between a man and woman, the love of a parent for a child. But while he loved all of his parishioners in a general way, and loved the world the Lord had created, he felt that he had missed out on a special loving relationship with one person. He longed to feel this and it seemed as though there was a hole in his heart where it should be. Then he angrily berated himself for being selfish. With all he had, his profession, knowing how to read and having the time to do so, plenty of food to eat, a beautiful church to live in, how could he complain? Surely it was a sin to wish for more.

When Bede opened the door, he met the dejected face of a young man. The monk could tell that this man ordinarily looked handsome, but currently was burdened with a pain so large that it filled his countenance. The man looked up and their eyes met. At that moment, Bede knew that they would be close friends.

"Welcome, stranger. How may I be of help?" asked Brother Bede.

"My name is Giles and I am here to ask about a burial. You don't know me, as I do not attend your services, but I live in Northborough," replied the seer.

"Come on in, and we can talk," said the monk, and they walked in to the church together. they walked companionably down the stone staircase to Bede's quarters, where he gestured to the seer to sit down.

Before doing so, though, Giles reached into his pocket and brought out the lifeless body of little West. He laid her with untold gentleness upon the table between them.

CHAPTER THREE

Bede could not find words. Naturally, living in Northborough he was aware of the diversity of magical creatures who lived in its denizens. Yet, he had never seen so exquisite an individual. She fit into his guest's hand, but was a fully-formed woman entirely made of gold. Her wings had begun to deteriorate. He felt so sad gazing upon her still body.

Giles began, "This is the fairy West. I had asked her to fly in that direction to find the Enchanted Cup. Morag was being harassed by Rhiannon and Cigfa. They wanted the Cup for no good reason other than to amuse themselves. When they hurt Morag's dog and threatened to take Monty away, I decided that I needed to help her. My three other fairy friends, East, North and South, flew in their directions but did not see the Cup. West must have traveled very far, but finally she found it, in America, whatever that is.

"The journey itself killed her. As soon as she flew in and rested a little, she told me and then died. She gave her life so that these terrible women could have some fun. I do not know if West is a Christian, but perhaps you would consent to burying her in the church graveyard."

"Of course, of course," began Bede. He wanted time to think about this, but things were happening very quickly. He would be happy to conduct the funeral. At least Giles and the other three fairies would attend. But what then? He was afraid that he would never see Giles again.

"Will you stay for some wine and cheese, Giles?" asked the monk, buying for time.

"Sure, I would love to, but don't try to convert me!"

"If that is your wish, I respect it." The monk knew that the best advertisement for his faith was the life of peace and happiness that he knew. No sermon could show how much God loved you, or how special you were in His eyes. Christians simply radiated it. Knowing that Heaven awaits you is so comforting that His people could relax while here on Earth. No one needed to worry or retaliate or feel hatred, because of God's all-encompassing loving-kindness, mercy and forgiveness. This made his job easy. He rose from the table and fetched some good quality wine and cheese. He brought along some thick country bread. Lighting a beeswax candle, they sat together, ate and drank.

Giles told Bede all about his gift. Bede enjoyed hearing the story, and told Giles a little about his own life. They made a plan for the funeral to be held the next day. Bede had a wooden box that they could use as a casket, and placed West reverently inside, cradled with soft wool and a small crucifix. They talked long into the night.

Chapter Four

Giles felt much better after talking with Brother Bede. After planning the funeral, he went to find Morag. She wandered outside of her cottage in the forest, gathering firewood for cooking.

"Hail, Morag," she called out to her. She stopped stooping and stood up straight.

"Giles, please tell me that you have good news. I have been waiting so long." After saying this she berated herself for her stiff words. Why could she never speak nicely to men? Why did she not say hello, ask about his health, thank him for his effort, first? No wonder she lived alone. She had no manners and thought only of herself. Perhaps it was time. She lived so many years taking care of her parents that she was just done with it. Now she took care of herself. Yet, this man was helping her and he did not even know her. He was good, she could tell. He was doing a favor without expectation of reward. Surely he must know that she had no way of repaying him.

"Morag, I bring mixed news. I wish that I could tell you that we will shortly find the Cup, but I've learned that it lives far away. I don't even know where, but it's somewhere in America, a place, I believe, straight west of here across the ocean. No one has ever seen it."

"No one?" she cried, and fell to the ground. At that moment, she did not think she would ever become free of the two witches. They would take her only companion away. Giles worried. He had no idea how to get to America, nor if any magic existed which could bring the Cup back to the shores of Albion. the situation truly seemed hopeless. Brother Bede could not think of a way there. The seer had only one idea.

"I have an idea, but am not confident that it will help. I will ask the king. If anyone knows, he will."

"Do you want to sit down, by the way? And, oh, yes, ask the king. That sounds good." Morag started walking back to her cottage with an armful of sticks. When they arrived, she lit a fire and began to boil water for tea--just like at their first meeting. She always did things backwards. She should have asked Giles to her home *first*, *then* talked about finding the cup. She most definitely lacked social skills. Once again, they sat in silence and sipped the herbal tea.

She added some honey. It was delicious. But this good taste could not take away the fear in Morag's heart. It just was not fair. The only thing she cared about in her life was her dog. Why did those witches have to target her for their fun? They had *everything*, even magical powers, could do *anything*, and picked on *her*, a woman alone in the forest who bothered no one.

Chapter Five

Giles slowly walked out of the basement. He reached the light; it was a sunny, happy day. He felt inside of his pocket, which the body of the fairy once filled. He felt the emptiness in his pocket. He reflected upon the situation, how the Christians say that when God closes a door, He opens a window. So losing West, he gained, he hoped, a friend. Maybe he would attend Mass next Sunday, just to see what it was all about. He had felt an attraction to the humble Bede.

Giles did not own a horse, so started walking toward the castle. As he walked, he hummed to himself, just a tuneless nonsense, to keep himself company. He turned around and walked toward the church.

"Brother Bede?" he called out.

The monk ascended the stairs, recognizing the voice. "Ah, you're back."

"Yes, I--I need to speak to the king, and do not feel comfortable. Perhaps, if you're not too busy, if, I mean, you have the time, your honor, I mean, sir, I mean, Brother Bede, would you please accompany me as I really have no idea how to do this alone."

Bede nodded his head. "I was hoping you'd ask," he said, and they began walking together toward Caradon Hall. Along the way, Giles pointed out some pretty spring flowers, and Bede would say, each time, "The goodness of the Lord has given these to us." Giles began to think that the monk was a little obsessed, he supposed, but in a good way. He was a good and kind person, and that was what mattered. They seemed to have a lot in common. Before long, the castle appeared on the horizon; they approached it, and knocked upon the great door.

Chapter Six

"Who goes there?" the chamberlain's deep voice bellowed.

The two young men looked at each other, neither knowing who should answer.

"It's…" they both began, then looked at each other and giggled.

"You go," said Bede, at the same time that Giles said, "You go."

"No, you go first," they said together, pointing at each other. "Oh dear, this is not going well," said Bede.

Giles replied, "I am not used to talking to royalty. I know Sir Ranaulf, but he seems like a regular guy. He was not born into wealth, so I feel comfortable with him. The others, well, I do not feel the same way."

"And I am?" wondered the monk.

"We have to do this, though," said Giles.

"Okay, I'll knock again and see what happens."

He did, and the chamberlain asked in his deep voice, "Who goes there?"

"It's only Brother Bede and Giles, here to ask a question, if you may."

"You may enter," Godfrey said, and the door slowly opened. The two young men stood in the great hall with the chamberlain. "Hello, and what is your business here?"

They looked at each other again, and giggled again.

"Please, this is the royal residence. I must ask for decorum."

Bede finally composed himself and explained, "We are trying to help a young peasant woman. You remember the Enchanted Cup?"

"Surely," replied Godfrey. How could he forget? It was that cup which brought the babe Ranaulf to Caradon Hall to be raised by the princesses.

"Ranaulf's sister must find it or Cigfa and Branwen will hurt her dog--and maybe even take him away."

"To be honest, that does not sound like the end of the world, Bede. Come back another time with a real problem."

Bede looked into the man's eyes. "Look, Godfrey. I am in the business of helping people. I like to make people happy. and right now, poor Morag is very stressed-out and sad. She loves that mutt more than anything in the world, and he's all she has. Please may we speak to the king about this?

"About what, exactly?" inquired Godfrey.

"About how to get to America."

"America? What is this A-mer-i-ca?" asked the chamberlain.

"It's this place, maybe an island like Albion, far away to the west. There are tales of it, but no European has ever seen it. Just think of the prestige! We'd be the first! Maybe they would name it after us! Godfreyville...Movanland..." explained Bede with enthusiasm.

"But it's called America already."

"For *now*, but if we are the founders, then they will have to respect that. We can draw a map and distribute it around Europe with the new name. So please could we meet with the king?" pleaded Bede.

"I guess, but I doubt he will want to help you. He is more concerned with the May Day festival that is fast approaching."

Both Bede and Giles thanked the chamberlain. They followed him to the king's office.

Chapter Seven

Morvan heard a knock on the door. He'd been enjoying some fine wine, and, truth be told, was feeling a little sleepy. "Ah, the heavy crown of leadership," he sighed to himself, and asked, sweetly, "Who is it?"

"It's me, Godfrey. I have a couple of visitors who want to ask you a question."

"You may enter," he said, remembering to use his kingly voice.

They came inside, while the chamberlain waited outside the door. "Be seated," Morvan instructed, and they sat down.

"How may I be of assistance?" Morvan asked, before letting out an un-regal burp.

The two looked at each other again, and giggled once again. They should have practiced how to do this. Neither one felt at ease in the presence of the king. But since Bede had some rank as a member of the clergy, and Giles none, Bede knew that he had to step up and begin.

"Your highness," began Brother Bede, "thank you so much for giving us this audience today, and on such short notice. But we have a matter of some importance to one of your subjects, the lovely Morag, sister of Sir Ranaulf. She needs to reclaim the Enchanted Cup, but the trouble is that it lies on a beach far away in America. We were hoping that you would help her to get there."

"Ha ha! America! Where on earth is that?" the king wondered jovially.

"Sire, it lies west of Northborough, far across the sea. No European has ever been there. We only know of its existence though legend and the flights of fairies like the one who gave her life to find the cup. Please help us!"

"What is in it for me, priest?" asked the king.

"I am not sure, sire, but perhaps this vast area of land might be named after you? I was thinking, 'Morvanland.'"

"I like the sound of it. But I don't know anything about navigating the seas. There is one person in Northborough, however, who does. His name is Captain Brendan. He pilots the *Cormorant*, the ship which keeps our merchant vessels safe from pirates. It also keeps us safe from invasion. He is one of my most valued subjects. If anyone can help you, it would be him."

"Thank you so much, your majesty. How do we meet this incredible man?" asked Bede.

"Just go to the shore. He stops in to port every once in a while for supplies. That is all I can do to help you. Don't even think about asking for money."

"We were about to ask you for some money."

"Fine! Take this and leave me alone." The king reached into a drawer and handed him a velvet pouch filled with gold coins. I was about to have a small, restorative nap. Even kings need their rest. It's not easy to rule a country, you know. And make sure that this new land is named after me. I do indeed like the sound of Morvanland. You are dismissed."

Giles and bede walked quickly out of the office. When the door closed behind them, they instinctively hugged. Then they looked into each other's eyes and could not help but burst out laughing. They had done it! The king was a mercurial character, funny and unpredictable, but deep down inside, a good man. They could only hope that Captain Brendan would be as helpful. It was getting late, so they decided to wait until the next day to find Captain Brendan. Besides, Giles had an idea.

Chapter Eight

The next morning dawned auspiciously. The sun in his eyes made Giles squint. After washing and breakfast, he took out his singing bowl. It once again was time to summon the fairies, this time, sadly, only three. The reverberating echo reached them, waking them as well. He dreaded having to tell them the news.

North, South and East flew in his window. They chatted happily, and Giles' heart broke. They did not know. "Come and sit with me," he told the golden sisters. They all easily fit onto his chair.

"Wait, where is West?" asked East.

"Yes, where is she?" North wondered.

"My dear girls," Giles began, "Your sister found the cup! She flew all the way to America, where it is located. It was so heavy that she could not carry it with her back to Albion, but now at least we know where it is. She has done a brave deed!"

"Yes, that's all very good, but *where is our sister?*" asked South, becoming worried.

"She did not survive the trip."

"NOOOOOOOO!" all three wailed in sorrow. They hugged each other in a tight circle. Their tears made tiny droplets of darkness onto the fabric covering Giles' chair. He tried to comfort them, but understood that it would take some time. They were, naturally, very close as quadruplets. He stroked their hair, and finally they calmed down.

"I will take you to the funeral today," he said. Just relax, have some honey-water. "I will understand if you do not want to do this, given what happened to West. But I have another mission for you and we could talk about it if you would like."

"Absolutely *not*," screeched North.

"You're *kidding*, right?" echoed South.

"Wait," said Giles. "Hear me out for a moment. This time I need to find a person, not an object. Morag needs Captain Brendan's help to get to America. I cannot imagine any other way. His ship, the *Cormorant*, patrols all of the coastlines of Albion for pirates. He travels with his first mate John to Eire and back, across the Narrow sea to Gaul and back. It's not that far. It's not dangerous. Please think about it, for her sake. If we stop now, West's death would be in vain."

"Well, if you put it *that* way," began East. "We perhaps could do it to finish her quest. I would hate to have her find the cup for nothing." Her sisters agreed. First, they attended the sweet and small funeral with Giles. Brother Bede conducted the sad ceremony. He had a deep and moving voice; when he sang the kyrie, gloria and alleluia, it filled Giles with something he had not felt before--an affinity to this Christian God? Or was it just love for

Bede? They went outside to the cemetery for the burial. The three fairies started flying in tight circles, consumed by grief. They screamed in high pitches. They circled in the air, flying randomly and aimlessly. They could not watch. It was too painful to witness their own, still young sister being placed into the earth.

Then, North, who was slightly more intuitive than her sisters, felt a strange presence. She looked over her shoulder to see a tall man, weathered and worn, approaching the cemetery. She flew to Giles and rested on his shoulder.

"Giles, who is that?" He could not believe his eyes. There, the mariner walked right toward them. Had he been summoned by the fairies? He would never know, but felt very relieved. After they had said their final blessings over the grave, Brother Bede and he both threw a handful of dirt upon it. The sisters cried noisily and hid their faces. There were three beautiful pots of flowers there. Each fairy flew over one as Giles and Bede placed them around West's tiny grave. North flew over the daffodil. South flew over the sunflower, and East flew over the yellow daisy. The golden flowers honored their golden sister. After more hugs, finally they huddled in Giles' pocket.

Giles walked toward the tall man wearing the navy wool coat.

End of Book V

Book VI

An Unlikely Friendship

Chapter One

"Hail Captain Brendan!" Giles called to him, not as happily as could be, because of his sorrow over West. Giles explained the quest to the captain. Captain Brendan looked older, but still handsome. He had been through so much, not only fighting pirates but also with the part of his body that was transformed into the sea by the mermaid, Maeve, many years ago.

The captain heard her calling for him. Brendan was sorely tempted to follow her, to live a life of ease in the sea, swimming wherever he wished, like a fish. But he ultimately remembered his duty to the king. Since he was a child, he had lived on a ship, and no one knew how to sail better than he. So good King Malcolm asked him to patrol the shores of Albion; pirates were a continual problem. Pirates from Eire, from Gaul and from the Norse lands overcame ships, but also landed on the sovereign shores and raped the women, killed the men and simply took over their homes and farmland. Without the reliable mariner, Albion would be much less safe. He decided in the last second to stay with his ship, but Maeve grew angry.

She cursed him, turning him into a sea monster. But he thought fast, and threw her a valuable coin. She stopped speaking in the middle of the curse! Luckily, only Brandon's eyes had become filled with sea water. They changed colors, reflecting whatever color the water was, such as pink rose at sunrise, blue on fair days, smoky-grey on cloudy ones, and purple at sunset. Sometimes they burned orange-red at the moment when the sun lay on the horizon. Brendan scared people who did not know him, people who did not know about the curse. So he only infrequently walked ashore. Every few weeks he needed to resupply his ship. Every few weeks he felt the draw of the church and Brother Bede.

Brendan blamed himself for his condition. He thought that he must be a very sinful man indeed, for entertaining the mermaid's promise. For wanting to follow her, if only for a few moments. For even *considering* giving up the grave responsibility he held protecting Albion's land and inhabitants. So he visited Brother Bede, confessed his sins, and received absolution. Bede was always glad to see the sailor, of course, but never understood the confession that always focused on an event long ago, for which he was certain the Lord had long ago forgiven this humble and hardworking soul.

Chapter Two

Twice in his life, Brendan had used a gift given to him by Maeve. He had the ability to dive into the water, turning himself into a sea creature. The first time that he used his ability was to save a sailor who had fallen overboard. That time, his first mate John had been horrified! But Brandon returned to his human shape once on deck, and explained the story to John. Then John became his best friend.

The second time that Brandon used his ability was to rescue the Enchanted Cup. Ranaulf was touring with him across the coast. Brandon knew how Ranaulf, the child of peasants, had come to live in Caradon Hall and be raised as a royal prince. The evil cup, with the face of a dragon, had been in his mother Matilda's family for decades. Matilda's family called her Maud. It had been passed down to the eldest daughter in each generation. Maud feared the cup greatly, for she had heard the stories of its power to transport those who drank from it far away. Relatives had lost their mind from drinking from the cup. One had even flown away, cackling like a witch.

She had placed the cup high upon the mantle above the fireplace, but when the family's cats played there, a swishing tail knocked it down. Maud had been outdoors working in the garden, and had not known that little Ranaulf had filled the cup with water, drank it, and disappeared. She never saw her son again.

Hugh and Maud moved away, away from the sorrowful memories, to another cottage, not far from there. A beautiful daughter, Morag, was born to them. Morag brought joy to the couple. She resembled her mother. She took care of her parents in their old age, and buried them when they died. However, as she grew older, she heard that her brother was alive! And that this brother lived like a prince in the royal castle! And this royal brother never contacted her, never bothered to say hello, never stopped by with perhaps some extra food or maybe a piece of cake. This knowledge taught the girl how cruel the world was, especially the world of men. She resolved to stay away from them whenever possible. All men did was cause pain and suffering. As far as she could see, they lived for their own pleasure and naught else.

Sir Ranaulf this, Sir Ranaulf that, she thought. It seemed as though he was always there for the rescue. The perfect chivalrous knight! *Pl-ease.* If they only knew. If they only knew how hard she had to work just to keep the family alive and together, to keep her mother from crying, to keep her father from falling into despair. Sure, he was a good knight. But he grew up in a castle, what do you expect? Life just wasn't fair. Not that she had the slightest inclination to live in a castle. *Never* would she do that. She just wanted to live her life alone.

Eventually, after years and years, her brother decided to grace her with his royal presence. She tried her best not to seem bitter. She tried her best to be a good hostess, as she had been taught. But in the end, it felt like a disappointment. He seemed sorry. She wanted him to be arrogant and unlikeable, but, unfortunately, he was a kind and caring man, just as people said. Well, they could say what they liked, he still abandoned his family.

Chapter Three

Giles caught Brendan's eye. Brendan looked up and waved. He walked along, and the two men embraced as they met. "It's been so long," said the seer.

"Too long," echoed the mariner.

At that time, Brother Bede approached them and invited them into the courtyard of the Church of the Holy Sandal to talk. He brought wine, cheese and good, hearty bread. Giles explained the mission to Captain Brendan.

"That would be a difficult journey," he began. "No one has ever sailed to the land called America, and come back to tell the story. Who knows what dangers lie between here and there?"

"So your answer is no, then," Giles said with disappointment. He bowed his head.

The sailor took a piece of bread and cheese. He thought carefully as he chewed. *These monks*, he thought, *really know how to make delicious food.*

"No, I didn't say that," he replied. "I need to speak with my first mate, John. See if he is willing to take this risk. I also have to ask the king to be relieved of my duties here in Northborough. But I am happy to help this young woman. It's no problem."

Giles took a piece of bread and bit into the salty crust. The monks had put some poppy and sesame seeds on the top, and he enjoyed the taste very much. The cheddar cheese was sharp, flavorful and on the mark. He sipped the excellent wine. Yes, no one made better food. He knew why his friend had a bit of an overhanging stomach.

Suddenly a shudder went through his body. He saw a vision of terror. Blurry, inexact, he could not tell what it was, but it frightened him. Was he sending this kind man to his death? He wished life could be easier. If he didn't have the sight, it would be so easy. Yet he'd been given this gift and wanted to use it for good, not for evil. Going to the dark side would be easy. But now, especially with his friendship with Bede, he wanted only to help people and make them happy.

Chapter Four

Brother Bede and Captain Brendan set off toward Caradon Hall. Recognizing them, Godfrey let them inside. However, King

Morvan said he didn't have the time to discuss nonsense. It was nearly Midsummer's Day! He had a ball to plan.

In reality, Morvan did not plan anything. His mother was gone, but she had set everything in motion already. He felt so down. He truly missed her, difficult as she could be. Yet his ultra-efficient multitasking mum had already planned the whole event. June twenty-fourth fell on a Saturday, next weekend. The finest food had been ordered, as well as the choicest beverages. Tables and chairs were being moved at that very moment. Using a chart, Bea had arranged space for dancing and space for the musicians.

His mother had also planned the decorations, which were currently in the midst of being created. Pastel ribbons of pink, yellow, blue and green connected the various elements in the grand ballroom, as well as hanging from the ceiling. Tailors had constructed flowers out of pastel fabrics. Each long, wooden board would be covered in a pale pastel tablecloth. Woolen yarn had been wound to make baby chicks and bunnies, ducks and lambs. Tiny fabric butterflies of lilac and pale salmon hung from thin threads. The start of summer was a joyous occasion, as everyone felt so energized and happy to see the sunshine and feel its warmth.

Yet Morvan moped. After much knocking, he finally responded, "Enter if you must."

The two young men explained the situation. Morvan only said, "Go away."

"But Your Majesty…"

"Well, fine. Are you going to ask for money now? Everyone asks for money eventually."

"No, actually we just wondered if…" said Bede.

"Oh, what do I care? You can go. Have your mate John do the patrolling instead. John stays. Brandon will need a ship, I suppose."

"Yes, Your Majesty," replied Brendan. "I guess you have heard about our quest."

"Am I not the king? Do I not know all that happens in Northborough? Just because Gondebald no longer lives here, that does not mean that I do not have spies and seers everywhere, like any sensible ruler?" he raged. "Now get out! I will only give you enough gold to survive comfortably, no more!"

The two young men hurried out the door as quickly as they could, closing it with a bang behind them. Once out, they looked at each other and let out the laugh that they'd suppressed inside. He was a character, their leader. But, deep down inside, he had a good heart. Perhaps what he needed was a queen. Perhaps that would calm his nervous spirit.

Chapter Five

Leaving Caradon Hall, they saw Goslar by the side of the road. "Goslar?" asked Brother Bede. He felt sorry for the elf since his mistress, Rhiannon, had died. Goslar lead a peripatetic life.

"Brother Bede! Good day to you! Would you like to purchase some holy dirt?"

Bede thought for a minute. He nudged Captain Brendan. "That is a curious question to be asking a priest, Goslar. We have many holy things here; holy water and saints' relics. Why would I want to buy some holy dirt?"

"I am glad that you asked," the elf began, in true salesperson's style. "You should buy the holy dirt as you never know when it might come in handy. Who knows what powers it may possess?"

"Where did you get this holy dirt?"

"The soil around the church of the Holy Sandal, of course, Brother Bede. It must be holy, as this is where your Lord Jesus Christ's sandal perished. The ashes are mixed with the ground, so it must be holy and have spiritual powers."

"Ah, now I understand," said the priest, feeling sorry once again. "How much for one vial?"

"A discounted price for you, father!" But then the little servant fell to the ground. He was too weak to stand.

Brother Bede and Captain Brendan quickly picked him up. They carried Goslar to the church. Giles came running and wanted to help, so he picked up the little sign,

Holy Dirt

Three Pence

and Goslar's meager belongings. They raced him to the church and lay him down. They tried to give him some water to drink. With a sigh of relief, Goslar woke up and was able to speak. He explained that he was homeless for so long, and he had not eaten a meal in days.

"Do not worry," said the priest. "From now on this is your home."

"But Father, I am not a Christian."

"I know my son. But a Christian sees the face of Jesus in all who suffer. It is my honor to take you in."

"Thank you, father. Do you have anything to eat?"

"Ha ha," he chuckled. "We eat very well here! Let us all have a meal as it is time for lunch." Giles noticed the little vial of holy dirt, and placed it in his pocket. He would save it, since, as Goslar said, you never know. Bede gave the gold pieces to Captain Brendan because, of course, you never know.

Chapter Six

Not wanting to waste any time, Giles walked to Morag's cottage. She assumed that it was bad news, and reluctantly let him in. But he explained that she and Captain Brendan could take the Cormorant, and some gold, and travel to America. Automatically she pictured this alpha male in her mind. *He must be completely full of himself*, she decided. *Captain of a ship! He'd barely notice her while he steered the vessel.*

Fine, she thought. She had never needed a man to keep her company. But it might be different on a ship, as she had her crops and garden here in Northborough, but what would she do there? The journey would take months, perhaps years. She wished that she knew how to read, but had never been taught. Surely the scenery would be worth watching; she would see things she had never seen before. The arrogant captain could stay on his side of the boat and she would stay on hers.

Then she remembered that she should be grateful. "Thank you, Giles. Have you 'seen' anything about this trip?" she asked, making little air quotes with her fingers. Indeed he had, but he did not want to share the frightening vision.

Instead he replied, "It's too far away and too far in the future for me to see anything. But I am sure that everything will go smoothly!" For he had a vision that woke him during his sleep. All of a sudden he felt so cold that even snuggling under woolen blankets, adding more blankets, and curling up into a ball could not warm him. By morning he felt better. But this had troubled him. He had never seen anything so white, but there it was, a blinding whiteness. Is America very cold and white? He didn't know and did not want to scare her. It wouldn't have mattered anyway, as he knew how strong-willed Morag was. Nothing would keep her from her quest.

Giles said goodbye to Monty. He had enthusiastically jumped upon his lap, but being a big dog, he pushed him off. Monty was content to sit at his feet and thump his tail instead. Giles pet the motley Monty and wished him safe travels.

After sharing some bread, cheese and tea, Giles left, informing the young woman to meet the Captain the next morning at the dock. The timing was auspicious, as spring would soon begin.

Chapter Seven

Morag carefully cleaned out her cottage. She threw all of her food into the compost. She gathered together her clothes, all of them, which fit into the sheet off of her bed. She made the sheet into a carrying case, tying the ends together at the top. She didn't know what else to take. Presumably the ship would have oil for lanterns, and candles and food. Morag never received an education, so not only could she not read, but she didn't know any geography. How long would this trip last? She could not imagine. All she knew was that they would travel west, toward the setting sun.

"Here, Monty!" she called, and he followed. She wondered if she would ever see her humble cottage again. Either way, she was prepared to do whatever it took to keep her beloved dog safe and close to her. He bounded up, following closely at her feet. Poor thing, he did not know what was coming. Do dogs like being on ships? Morag didn't know. So much about the upcoming adventure was unknown to her. Yet she didn't feel fear. She just was not that kind of girl. Monty licked her hand as they walked toward the shore.

Today she wore her warmest dress, even though it was April, and the weather had begun to change. It was her heaviest, so she didn't want to carry it. The two best friends walked along, Morag keeping her chin up as, like on that fateful day when she met the two witches, her braids swung in the wind.

She spotted the Cormorant after a while. As they approached, she also spied a dark figure. *That must be the captain*, she thought. When Morag reached him, it was as if a jolt of lightning ran through her lithe body. She did not trust this new feeling. It was not the same as how she felt for Monty, but a different kind of affection, an animal spirit, a spark. The most independent young woman in Northborough had no intention of falling for any mere man. Yet here it was happening. She vehemently fought this emotion off.

Book VII

A Dilemma for a King

Chapter One

King Morvan woke up with the sun in his eyes. He loved to sleep in. In fact, he slept in every day. Why not? He was the king. No one could tell him what to do. He loved that about being king. No one could tell him what to eat, what to wear. Well, there was that *one* time when the barons forced that ridiculous bill of rights, the, what-did they-call-it, the Carta of Northborough on him. But this was not the time to dwell on negative thoughts. It was May Day, the day of the ball; May the first.

His primary responsibility was to show up, make a speech, and enjoy some good food and wine. He wanted his people to be happy. He was a benevolent and beneficent ruler. He loved that about himself. His people were happy and well-fed; they admired him. The ball would be a success. Sure, only the bourgeoisie were coming, but the hoi polloi had plenty of fun on their own. He couldn't invite everyone, could he? There wasn't enough room in the castle.

After washing and having his breakfast, he received reports from the New Order of the Pegasus. Each knight told him what was going on in the land. The knights were more or less ministers of state. One handled foreign relations, one law and order, one agriculture, one defense. One knight looked after health and another economics and business. They respectfully asked his advice, which Morvan sagely dispersed.

Next, the king read the letters of petition. Goodness, every day there were a pile of those. "Please, Your Majesty, my ox has died and I need a new one or I will perish!" "Please, Your Majesty, my neighbor is stealing my crops! Will you stop him?" "Please, Your Majesty, I cannot afford to pay my taxes, may I have an extension?" and so on and so on.

"Please, Your Majesty, my wife is troubled by an evil spirit and I don't know what to do." "Please, Your Majesty, I cannot afford health care for my child who is gravely sick and I fear may die. Blah, blah, blah."

Can they not solve any problems on their own? Still, he enjoyed helping them. He thought of them as his helpless little children. After he dispensed some favor, a doctor, a new animal, a spell-breaker or priest, he felt so *good!* It really made his job rewarding. He felt grateful for his position. After all, not just anyone is born to be king, and not just anyone can rise to the responsibility. He just had inherited the right personality to rule. He felt that he was the best combination of his mum and dad.

Morvan could be decisive like his mum. Like her, he saw himself as good-looking and intelligent too. Like his father, he had a big heart and humanity. A sense of humor. the more he thought about it, the more he realized that he was born for this role. No one really could rule quite as well as he. He gave himself a little pat on the back. It was time to get ready for the ball.

Chapter Two

Ophelia could not really describe the splendor. Caradon Hall had been decorated with a spring theme for

May Day, the first of May, and it looked so beautiful! The aquamarine sky matched her bright blue eyes. *What a perfect day*, she mused. Yet she could not get herself excited for the ball. It was just another job for her. After her parents died, she had to fend for herself, and that meant dancing at the local pub in town. She waited tables, serving ale, mead, wine, and food. She danced, and that was what brought the customers in, her boss told her. He thought that complimenting her would compensate for the ridiculously low wages he paid her, but it did not. But what was she to do? She needed the money and the room upstairs that he let her live in. So she kept her mouth shut and did her job, quite well, thank you very much.

  The smell of the food was intoxicating. Ophelia knew other girls who had to work as prostitutes in order to survive. She felt horribly for them, but in her job she at least could keep the men's hands off her and a small piece of her dignity. Let them try to touch her, and she'd smile and slap their hand away. But in a nice way. She had to keep them coming back. Working at the pub meant that she ate well and never had to worry about hunger. Luckily for her, the owner was an honorable man and did not abuse her.

Guests arrived and began to eat and drink. Musicians played. Her employer, the Queen Mother Beatrice, had left. Not just gone upstairs, but left Northborough. She had left Albion. She was going to Rome with some weird goth stranger from the east to try to get backing for his idea. This deranged man believed that the earth revolved around the sun. Ha ha! Perhaps he has been bewitched or has taken some herbs that made his brain turn into mush. There's no accounting for taste, as they say, so Beatrice has left with him.

Bea's poor husband, the long-suffering Mesmin, stays in his room now. He has the servants bring him his drinks. He barely eats. For years, he gave up alcohol, but the day his wife left him was the day he began his addiction once again. He had tried so hard to make her love him. He knew that he was not attractive, but he was a skilled wizard and could give her everything she wanted.

Except becoming queen. She had always wanted to be the queen, and he failed her more than once. Her third idea was to become the *mother of the king*, and in this, she succeeded. But Mesmin was always a figure in the background of the beautiful and ethereal princess. He felt like a bit part in one of William Shakespeare's plays. She had the lead; he only appeared in one scene. She is Viola in *Twelfth Night;* he is the First Officer. He fades into the background. He is a bystander in her fabulous life.

Chapter Three

Events proceeded smoothly even without the Queen Mother. The guests were having so much fun! Finally King Morvan graced us with his presence. Ophelia watched him from the shadows. He was a fine-looking young man. He must have taken after his mother. She tried to quell the little flutter her heart insisted upon performing, like one of the pastel butterflies decorating the room. She was basically a barmaid who could dance. Big deal. She knew that she was a nobody and never would marry a king. But a girl can dream, right?

Her impression of Morvan did not match her expectations. She had imagined him resembling the taciturn father, who sat with his cup and head down at the main table. When the King entered, it was like the room lit up. He had an upbeat demeanor, and seemed to be enjoying the music, food and drink. He wore his crown as if he were born with it. His whitish-blond wisps of hair grew like vines around its circle. For this occasion, he donned the rich crimson robe lined with ermine that royals seem to love, setting off his pale blue eyes. White tights covered his muscular legs and pointed slippers embroidered with gold graced his feet. He looked a little humorous, she thought, but dared not say anything aloud. Ophelia heard a tambourine beat thrice; this was her signal to go.

Ophelia danced as she always did; it was naught but a job for her. Or perhaps she lied to herself. Perhaps, in reality, she danced with more agility, more enthusiasm, and more grace than usual. After all, she was performing in the royal residence, not the village pub. Her hair flew behind her. The harp could not play fast enough for her moves. And then she saw him; the king was following her with his eyes.

As she expected, after the glorious May Day ball, he called for her in his room. What could she do? She could not disobey the king. It put her in a bad situation. He held inordinate power over her. It was not as if she could say "no." She should have thought of this beforehand. Men of power always got their way; it had always been thus. Their superior strength meant that they could easily subdue an unwilling female. And in Morvan's case, he had the power of his knights on his side. She felt devalued, but had to follow him. There was nowhere to hide.

But she was not exactly upset about it. Not exactly. There would be an uproar. She would demand that he marry her to preserve her honor. If Beatrice were there, she would have prevented it. A commoner, and a barmaid at that! Not in a million years would her precious son marry this trash.

But Beatrice was not around, and Mesmin acquiesced to the marriage. Mesmin seemed happy for them; he really did not care. He was so sad that he did not care about anything anymore. "Sure, marry the barmaid. Whatever," he said. Ophelia knew that the wedding had to occur soon, just in case the Queen Mother returned. There were plenty of ladies-in-waiting to help.

Chapter Four

Cigfa and Branwen had mixed feelings. They loved occasions of all kinds (another party!), but it would have been better if this king had found someone with royal blood. What on earth would they talk about with her? What would they have in common? Maybe they could make her into a real queen. Maybe they could teach her everything that she should know about hair, makeup, jewelry, shoes and clothing. They could teach her courtly manners and how to speak as if she were brought up an aristocrat.

"This could be fun, Branwen," said Cigfa.

"I have been so bored that this is *just* the little project we have been looking for! Teasing Morag and her pathetic little mutt has lost its lustre for me," Branwen replied.

"Surely, for me as well, sister."

"She's leaving, you know."

"Who is leaving?"

"Morag, the country lass. She's getting on the Cormorant to fetch the Enchanted Cup for us."

"Well, that is kind of her. Is she taking the pet with her?"

"Yes, of course. I think she is terrified we would kill the hairy beast."

"Would we?"

"Branwen, we would do no such thing. It was only to motivate her that we tortured Montgomery. What a pretentious name for a dog!"

"I have to agree, Cigfa. She needs to be brought down a notch."

"Where did you say she was sailing off to? I am getting confused between Morag and Beatrice. Why can't they just stay here and amuse us?"

"I feel as if I am your assistant, sister. Bea is headed off to Rome with her tall, dark and handsome Mikolaj. Morag is sailing to America with Captain Brendan and the mutt, because we ordered her to give us the Enchanted Cup...or else."

"But Branwen, that could take months...years! I cannot wait that long, can you? Could we do something?"

"Why not? Let's make the wind blow behind them, so that the ship almost flies like a bird!"

"How fun! What a great idea, Branwen! But won't they be *afraid*?"

"Mortals *should* be afraid of magic. Don't worry; they might even enjoy it. They will get home faster."

"We're so clever, aren't we, Branwen?" said Cigfa, hugging her sister tightly.

"We are, Cigfa, aren't we the cleverest?"

Chapter Five

A June wedding was planned for the king and Ophelia. She enthusiastically submitted to her future great-aunts' planning. That was the good part. The sad part, she thought, was how distant Morvan seemed. The night of the ball he was attentive and affectionate. No more. It was like he lived inside of a bubble, or within a perpetual reverie.

"Is something troubling you, dearest?" she asked.

"No, I'm fine, and you?" he asked with good manners, but distance.

She felt frustrated. Naturally she had gone back to the pub and resigned. She was given one of the many extra rooms in the castle, on the other side from the young king. When she brought a small sack with her belongings to her room, Cigfa and Branwen promptly threw them in the poor bin.

"Silly girl! You're pretty but not too brainy, are you? We will give you all *new* clothes! Your bed will have all *new* sheets! If there are no precious enough jewels for you, we will conjure them!" Cigfa announced.

Branwen said, "My specialty is emeralds; I will make you a set of earrings and a necklace! As old Saint Hildegard said, 'All the green of nature is concentrated in the emerald.' It is the stone of springtime."

"I will fashion a ring for you in amethyst. It is the symbol of royalty, so just perfect for you, our future queen!" Cigfa added.

Ophelia felt like she finally had a family. After her parents' death she had experienced loneliness. Not that every patron of the pub wouldn't become her betrothed, but she had standards. She had no interest in living with a drunkard for the rest of her life. "Thank you so much, Branwen and Cigfa."

The two witches wanted her as an ally. It was too easy. A simple gift of jewelry and she was theirs. You never know when her debt of friendship might come in handy.

Chapter Six

"I just love weddings, don't you?" Cigfa asked Branwen as she plaited Ophelia's hair into two braids on either side of her head. Then she wrapped them around and secured them. Her long brown hair was thick and shiny, and she stood with a new straight back, thanks to her training. No slouching! No stringy hair! Branwen had brushed the girl's hair a hundred strokes to make it shine. It was enjoyable seeing the former barmaid turn into a queen before their eyes. Ophelia cleaned up nicely! She tucked flowers into the braids like pearls.

Morvan would have asked her father for permission to marry the pretty lass, but he had died young, of illness and exhaustion. He asked Mesmin, and the easygoing mage said that it was fine, as long as he was happy. But Morvan looked anything but happy.

"Dearest, why are you so melancholy?" Ophelia wondered the day before the nuptials.

"I don't want to tell you."

"But Morvan, you must tell me or I will not go through with this. If we are to have a good marriage, one like that between my parents, God rest their souls, we must be completely open and honest with each other. You must tell me what troubles you." She looked at him, and noticed his soft lips. She reached over and gave him a kiss. He enjoyed it very much. His future bride smelled so good now that his aunts had gotten a hold of her. They made her bathe and used their salts and fragrances in the water. She washed her mouth and brushed her teeth now with their compounds. It was *heaven* to kiss her, but he could not shake his anxiety.

"It is horrible," he said.

"Please tell me," she implored, looking into his eyes and holding his hands in hers.

"I worry that you will no longer wish to marry me…"

"Don't be ridiculous, Morvan. You have captured my heart and I cannot escape from you. I want to help."

"It's a dream I had, Ophelia." She looked into his eyes to show that she had given him her full attention. So he continued, "I murdered that interloper Mikolaj. He was sleeping in our castle and I snuck up to him and pierced his heart with a long knife. He jumped up at me! I had to stab him over and over. You cannot believe how much blood there was! But then he lay back, his eyes accusing me. I still see those eyes. But I take it as a message. I am meant to kill him. These images haunt me constantly. Over and over I replay the dream in my mind."

Ophelia was horrified. She had not expected that Morvan could think such thoughts, even unconsciously. Is he capable of violence? Would she be safe if she married him? Did he see himself stabbing her, as well, as she slept? Now she felt anxiety cover her like a blanket. But what could she do? He was her king. She reached out to him and rubbed his shoulders and back.

"There, there," she consoled him. "It's only a dream! Probably the trick of some witch or sorcerer. Someone wants to cause trouble and is planting this idea in your head."

"But the problem is, Ophelia, I really want to do it."

Chapter Seven

Ophelia may have only been a country barmaid, but she understood people. She saw how her betrothed was troubled by this dream and violent thoughts. Since there was no getting out of this marriage now, all she could do was to try to help Morvan.

"My love, all men dream of violence. It is in your blood, and yours especially, being royal. Are not kings the ones to declare war? Do not leaders send their valiant young men into battle? Perhaps it's time for some jousting or hunting? To get it out of your system, you know?"

While Morvan considered these very excellent suggestions, a dark cloud encompassed his brain.

"But what if Mikolaj *deserves* to die? Look what he has done to my father, who clings to life by a thread! The sunshine, the spark has disappeared from his eyes. He was so in love with my mother; he would do anything for her. He would give her whatever she wanted. He only wished her to be happy, and now she has left him for that alien. I want to kill him, Ophelia, I do!"

"Yes, but they are gone now, and you would never find him. Perhaps if he came back, that would be your opportunity. In the meantime, could we just have a beautiful wedding day?"

"When I look at the walls of our castle, I see the bloody knife hovering in the air, as if enchanted. It drips scarlet drops! How can I concentrate?"

"Your father is heartbroken now, but what would he want you to do? Mope and be weary? No, he would want you to continue to be the excellent ruler that you are. The kingdom is at peace; the people are well-fed and happy. That is due to your own leadership, as well as his role model as your father. Go to him, Morvan, and talk. Explain how much you love and admire him."

Chapter Eight

The next morning, Morvan made the trek to his father's room upstairs. He knocked; no answer. He walked in anyway. The door was unlocked. Looking up, he saw the man who fathered him at his table, studying a dusty book of magic. Not that he had to, since he was a good magician. He just enjoyed reading the old spells and imagining them in his head. Right now he looked at a moon stave, which kept away ghosts. All you had to do was carve the symbol into a fox pelt and color it with blood from your right index finger. A similar one is carved into a dog's spine on the third day of a new moon. You then lay beneath it and when you slept, you could dream anything you wanted to.

"Greetings, son! Or should I say, 'your majesty'"?

"Father, you know we are too close for that."

"Come, have a seat! Would you like some wine?

"Sure, father. How have you been?" Mesmin poured

a cup for his son and refreshed his own. "I came for advice. I came here to talk to you about that. I know you miss mother so much. I can see it in your eyes."

"No, son, I'm fine, really. Never better. How is the fair Ophelia?"

"Father, I don't want to chit-chat. I am here for a serious purpose. I've been troubled by horrible dreams. I've seen a ghost!"

"Ghosts are a part of our world, son. they are everywhere! They are in the room with us now as we speak! Sometimes, when they want to communicate with us, they will appear as a solid form. Sometimes, as an ethereal, mist-like being. The Christians even believe in them, although they call them by different names, such as angels, archangels, devils and demons. They pray for the souls of their dead, and what are those? Ghosts! The goal of the ghost is to arrive in Heaven. Imagine every person who has ever lived on earth. Their ghosts inhabit our spaces, and enjoy watching us. They miss their bodies, I think, and like to imagine what they would do in our place, were they still here. I would not be afraid of ghosts, then."

"This is fascinating stuff! Why have you never told me these things before? Why was I not taught this from my tutors?"

"I believe that they may have feared that you would join the new religion and turn your back on the old ways, the ways of magic."

"But the two systems coexist very well! Some go to church, others practice at the place of the standing stones or in the moonlight. We respect each other," the king replied.

His father answered, "Son, as the future ruler, it was important to your mother and I that you, that…" and here he began to cry. He put his head down on the board and sobbed. Mesmin mumbled in a small voice, "Bea, Bea, Bea…"

Morvan explained to his father, "Father, this is what I'd like to speak with you about, actually." He rubbed Mesmins back, trying to sooth him. "In my dream, I killed the foreign intruder. I stabbed him with a dagger until he stopped moving. There was blood everywhere. I am deeply troubled by this dream, wondering if it is a prescription for action, for what I need to do as king. I know they have left, but I am sure that you could find Milkolaj with magic."

Mesmin thought about this. Then he responded, "Son, I am sorry that you are troubled by this dream. Let me think about how we can end it. In the meantime, please don't worry about me. I am fine, really." Here, he burps. "Even if Mikolaj were dead, the point is that Beatrice the Fair no longer loves me. That is what has crushed my heart. If she were here next to me, it would almost be worse, since I would know she would be faking her emotions. It's okay, Morvan. You are a good son. I will work on a spell to relieve you of this dream."

Morvan was even more troubled now. His father clearly suffered from sadness, and depression. The drinking was only a symptom. Loneliness was the disease. He had always been closer to his mother, with her *elan*, her *joie de vivre*. But no more. Now he felt his father's sadness, and bonded with him. He would do whatever he had to to make him feel better.

In the meantime, he secured some St. John's Wort, a herb that worked sometimes to help with sadness. It's pretty yellow flowers were collected by healers, women who made drugs, dried and crushed. Then they were made into a tea bag. He got his father some hot water and honey and they sat for a while while Mesmin drank. So as not to be rude, Morvan had some tea, too. However, in the back of his mind, he could not stop the thought that an herbal tea would never be able to bring happiness back to his father's life.

Book VIII

Power for Warmth

Chapter One

The Cormorant swung left to right; it swished in the waves. This was not like the coast of Albion. Now they were out in the ocean, in deeper, colder water. The strangest thing was how fast she skimmed the sea. Captain Brendan wondered if this were normal, or if some witchcraft were at work. It didn't seem possible for their simple wooden craft, lashed with a strong beam and sail, to travel at this speed. they pushed forward like breath blowing out a candle at bedtime.

    Morag was thinking the exact same thing. Though she had never been on a boat, let alone in the vast ocean, she could tell that this experience was paranormal. Naturally, her mind focused on Cigfa and Branwen. Who else? They were anxious for their little cup.

    She had to admit it was more beautiful at sea than she could imagine. Each sunrise, every sunset, seemed larger than the whole world. At night, when Brendan brought out his lute and sang softly, they watched the stars overhead. The other thing that she had to admit, that went against her whole being, was that she was getting feelings of affection for the young man. When it felt right to lean her body against his as they sat upon the deck one warm night, he did not move away.

These feelings surprised her. She knew other girls lost their heads over boys. They forgot about important things in life and simply longed for marriage and children. She looked at men. Did they long for marriage and children? No! All of them wanted adventure, challenge, glory! Why did it have to be different if you had the misfortune of having been born a female? It was so unfair. Now, here she was, on an adventure, and her mind goes to the unthinkable place...of wanting to marry this handsome sailor.

Brendan hardly slept. Partly this was due to having to steer the ship. He was teaching Morag how to do this, so that they could take turns. It felt good to have a co-pilot. But he was also troubled by thoughts of longing for her. He had heard about her independent nature. Would she be offended if he tried to hold her hand? To kiss her? It was pretty much all he thought about. But when she leaned into him, he realized that yes, she was thinking the same thing as he was. He was worried that it would be taking advantage of her, as she had nowhere else to go, trapped upon this ship. But now he felt emboldened, and they leaned against each other for support.

Chapter Two

No one knew what existed on the other side of the ocean. Captain Brendan had heard stories, of course. He'd heard of monsters and sea creatures, mysterious voices and killer winds and rocks. But no human had traveled to America and back, so this was all speculation.

They had not planned on encountering islands, but were so grateful that they did. Usually all they had to eat was fish they caught over the side of the boat. The first island they met was full of plants and animals. Brendan used his bow and arrow to provide meat, which they roasted on a fire on the beach. Birds sang in the trees, and rivers provided fresh water that they refilled the ship's barrels with. They enjoyed lush fruit, and named the island "Paradise." They stayed for three days and three nights.

Fearfully, they encountered Judas Iscariot sitting upon a very large, grey-black rock in the ocean. They asked him why he was there. He replied that God allows him out of Hell on Sundays. He was cold and wet, clearly suffering even though he was not down below. Captain Brendan let Judas hang out with them on the boat for the day. The one who betrayed Christ was so grateful--he played with Monty and jumped and ran. Still, he had to leave at the end of the day.

One island was full of sheep, which meant meat again. Strangely, a single dog wandered around. Monty was so happy, not only to be able to run around again, but to meet a kindred soul. Another weird thing about Sheep Island was that there were tables left out with bread and water on them, which they took along onto the ship. Even stale bread was better than none. They stayed for three days and three nights.

Sailing along, they passed a pillar, as if stuck into the sea. This pillar was covered in fishing nets.

The next island they landed upon housed fourteen monks. This was a special surprise! Brendan and Morag attended Mass with the monks on Sunday. The monks do not speak, but the visitors understood nevertheless. The Island of Jasconius had vineyards and they feasted upon fresh grapes. The monks gave them wine, which they kept on the ship for future sustenance. Finally, they witnessed a battle between a gryphon and a chicken, and the chicken won, eating the gryphon. Now that was unexpected!

On the next island was a well. They walked up to the well, which had a bucket tied to a string, and turned the wheel which brought it up. After drinking the water, which tasted fresh and delicious, they fell into a deep sleep of three days and three nights.

After awakening, they sailed on toward a mist, which turned out to be a group of volcanic islands. They had black sand and black stiff sides, so had to keep going. Dolphins accompanied them as they traveled. But in the distance there was an island so large that there was no navigating around it.

Chapter Three

Therefore they landed upon it. This island, *or was it land?* had a white sand beach. It seemed deserted and beautiful. They descended the gangplank and splashed in the shore. Monty was, as always, jubilant to be upon *terra firma* once again. The first strange thing they witnessed was a snowy owl flying above, calling, "Who, who?" The second was a white rabbit nibbling upon some carrot tops. Brendan asked, "Morag, why would there be white creatures here upon this warm and sunny island?"

She thought about it, but could not come up with a good answer. "I've never seen these white animals before, but we have come across so many unusual things upon our journey, that I am not really worried."

So they put together their blankets within the thick woods, and went to sleep, watching the stars above twinkle and wink. Their bodies snuggled tight, their mutual warmth wrapping them inside of a deep sleep.

Morning brought a chill. Snow was falling! How could this be after such a warm day? Morag had never seen snow before; she and Monty examined the individual flakes and rejoiced in their beauty. But soon she felt cold. Morag and Brendan went back up the plank to the Cormorant for their coats. The temperature dropped and they made the decision to leave. There must be a way around this island.

But when they returned to the ship, it was trapped in ice. Now they were afraid.

What kind of magic was this? They soon learned when a white chariot approached, driven by two white horses. "Greetings, I am Queen Frostleigh," the stunning woman with long, pure white sparkly hair said to them, descending and approaching. Brendan and Morag felt a chill penetrate their bones. Neither had ever felt so cold. "I am so happy to have visitors! I infrequently have visitors! I like to show hospitality to my guests, so I have provided you with a winter landscape!"

They worried that this woman was out of her mind. Who does that? Don't people usually bring a bottle of champagne or pastries? They also noticed that beneath her white gown she was barefoot. This tipped them off to the fact she must be a witch, as no one else could stand this cold.

Chapter Four

"Hi, Queen Frostleigh. We are Captain Brendan and Morag, along with her dog Montgomery, and we journey to find an artifact. We come in peace wanting to hurt no one. But this cold is more than we can survive. I feel my fingers and toes becoming numb, dear lady. Please can you make it warm again?" Brendan pleaded.

As he spoke, he looked up to see the tree branches becoming covered in ice. While lovely, they scared him. He was in charge. He was the captain. Two other lives depended upon him to get them home safely, and now he wondered if he could fulfill his mission or not.

"Make it warm? Just like that? Like a little trick or something? Who do you think I am? Do you believe that I waste my magical powers on trifles? No, I have frozen you for a reason. You and the girl will freeze to death, and your bodies will lie forever here, and no one on this earth will ever know."

"*Please*," Brendan begged. "Why are you doing this to us? Have we harmed or offended you in some way, your majesty?"

"Maybe I am just jealous of you. Maybe I want you to suffer, as I suffer. I'm stuck here on this island for my entire life. I'm the ruler! Where else could a female rule? It's always kings, kings kings. The eldest boy becomes the next ruler while the girls sit back and watch. At least here I am in charge! No one tells me what to do. I fell into the crystal lake as a child, and when I came out, I found that I could do things other humans could not do."

Brendan said, "I understand, your highness. I completely commiserate with you. But what is the crystal lake?" He shivered, becoming colder with each passing moment.

She replied, "Inside of this island is a shiny white lake, which reflects the colors of the sky, becoming pastel shades of pink and blue and green. I didn't realize that it was enchanted, and, reaching for a fish inside, I fell in. And now, here I am, able to cast spells and do all kinds of things that you should be envious of me for, but then again, I am angry and alone. You, on the other hand, are not alone. You have something I will never have--love."

Morag and Brendan looked at each other. they had not used the word "love," even in their heads. Could that be the emotion they felt? Their hearts started to beat in a shaky, fibrillating way. Were they in love?

Brendan's protective instinct kicked in again. He could not let Morag die. An idea appeared in his head..."Queen Frostleigh, have you ever wished that you could swim in the ocean--to be free? If you are marooned on this island, there is a way..."

The queen was shocked by this revelation. For one thing, she did not expect the mere human to bargain with her. For another, she never imagined that she would be able to leave the island. So she asked him, "What are you proposing, Brendan?"

Chapter Five

Brendan explained to her his power to change himself into a sea monster. What he did not include was the part about losing five years of his life every time he used it. "I am offering you this gift I have--to become free! But in exchange, you must warm us up and allow us to leave. You must melt the ice surrounding the Cormorant so that we can continue on our quest."

The beautiful white queen thought about this. More so than the freedom, the ability to gain extra powers sounded good. She craved even more powers. Wealth meant nothing to her, as she lived alone. But to writhe and move like a fish, to breathe in the water, how exciting! She wondered if it were a trick...but then realized that she had nothing to lose. If the sailor had no such power, he would just die anyway. However, if he did, then she would have it for herself. So she acquiesced.

"This had better not be a trick, Captain. But come here, hold onto my hands." they stood facing each other, arms entwined to the elbows. She gazed into his eyes, and he felt her warmth come into his arms and eyes. Her eyes became bright red like a cardinal's. Then the warmth turned hotter and hotter. His arms burned, smelling like a roast on the fire. And tragically, his eyes became burnt as well. He could no longer see; Brendan was blind. He screamed out, cursing the white witch. She had taken his sight along with the gift. He fell to the ground, and Morag rushed to his side.

"Why did he think nothing would happen? Everything has a cost," Frostleigh hissed, "and if you want off of my island, this is the price I will extract from you. Otherwise you will freeze to death. you and the girl, and the mutt."

Morag tried to ease the pain in his arms but he called out in even greater pain. She watched as the ice around the Cormorant melted. They could not get off of this horrible island soon enough. Monty barked at the white witch, knowing that she was evil. Morag helped Brendan to get up. Hopefully the blindness was temporary, because if it was not, she would be the one steering the ship, and she had no idea how to get to America.

The only good side of this was that they were free to leave. Brendan leaned upon her, and they staggered toward the ship. Monty, not understanding, walked close behind. Brendan said nothing. It was up to Morag to set the sail in the other direction, moving to the left, or south, to go around this large island. She was always an independent woman, and would make the most of this. She would make it work. Her heart wasn't really in it, though. Here this good person, her beloved Brendan, had been blinded by an evil witch. How much more his life was worth than even that of her companion Monty. She felt terrible. He must hate her. All of this was her fault, and if she had just let Cigfa and Branwen have Monty, none of this would have happened.

Chapter Six

After they left, Brendan stopped talking. He wouldn't say a word. Morag became really concerned. She held his hand and led him around. She wished that she knew how to read, so that she could read to him. She wished that she knew how to play the lute, so that she could soothe him through a song. She actually picked up the instrument and tried to make some harmonious music, but all that came out were discordant sounds. She wanted to crush the lute, but held back, knowing that Brendan loved it. All she could do was to hope that he would take it up again when he felt better.

Once the Cormorant made it around the island, she watched as it became green again. She thought about how life was not fair. She thought about how she loved being alone before, and how much her heart creaked, moaned and burst for Brendan. Now he was blind because of her. His arms, she could nurse back to health. But she had no remedy for his beautiful eyes, the eyes made of seawater that changes color to match the uppermost layer of water. Was there ever a human such as him? *No*, she said to herself, *never*. He is one of a kind.

Morag thought about how the bad people always seemed to come out on top. *Why was that?* She remembered how the Christians said that in the next life, you would be rewarded for your goodness, but not necessarily in this life. She wondered if that were true. But how could anyone know? It was only speculation.

She knew that she loved Monty. But, against her will, she began to cry. Could it be that she loved Brendan, too? Loving a man, she thought, never turned out well. She felt a new protectiveness of this good man. She hoped that it was not too late for him to love her back. He heard her tears and turned in her direction. They held each other and fell asleep.

The next morning, the tailwinds began to blow again and they rushed across the waves. The boat seemed to steer herself, just pointing west toward America. She checked the steering once in a while, caught and roasted some fish, and brought Brendan water and meals. She washed their clothes in the seawater. Time slowed down. Her heart was not in this journey, and she didn't feel good about it. A foreboding came over her. She wished that she could go back, back to Albion, to Northborough, to her little humble cottage. She wished that she could go back in time to before Cigfa and Branwen entered her life.

One thing she did not wish for was to go back to living without her beautiful Captain Brendan.

Chapter Seven

Was the Cormorant guided by magic? Did Cigfa and Branwen somehow secretly control the boat? Morag could not be sure, but she suspected it. The large land mass ahead had to be the mysterious America. A voyage that should have taken months had taken days. She believed that America lay ahead because of all of the birds in the air. So many birds, large and small, must live on a continent rather than an island. Then there was the dove, holding a small olive branch in its mouth, a sure sign of land. Hadn't Noah said that in the Bible?

It didn't really matter, though. The boat made it ashore, and Morag grabbed Brendan's hand. Monty romped right behind, again overjoyed to get off the tilty ship and onto land. Like in a dream, they walked together toward the thickly wooded area just past the beach. They would sleep there tonight.

Brendan heard Morag softly crying. This would not do. He loved her but was deeply ashamed that he could no longer see and was at her mercy. Surely, without her help, he would die. But the sound of her sobs brought back his will to speak. "Dear Morag, please don't cry." They snuggled together under his thick wool coat. He clumsily tried to wipe the tears from her eyes. "It will be better, and we will find your cup, I can feel it. West could not be wrong."

She sniffled and brought her body next to his. His warmth filled her with happiness and hope. "Yes," she replied. "It will get better."

In the morning they began to walk along the shore. There were many interesting objects marooned there, such as skeletons of large fish and beautiful seashells. Her long braids swished in the wind. Her dress flew away from her legs, and she felt so free, but she was so far away from home, and did not even know where she was, exactly. It was somewhere west of Albion. That is all she could understand.

"I feel badly that I cannot help you in finding the cup," Brendan told her. She was so relieved that he was talking again. Not much, but talking.

"I don't care! I feel so much better that you are beside me. I don't think I would have the courage to handle this on my own. My whole life I have envisioned myself as the most independent woman. I wanted no one's help. I may have had a bit of a chip on my shoulder because of the cup and Ranaulf's fame and fortune. But since I've met you, I feel differently. I feel vulnerable. This is a brand-new feeling for me. It's both frightening and thrilling."

She reached over to him and stroked his cheeks. "Thank you, Captain Brendan, for being here with me."

Chapter Eight

They walked and walked. Monty splashed in the waves. The warmth felt good. Her head down, she kept her eyes out for the cup. And then she noticed something shiny, glinting in the sunlight and reflecting it. She led Brendan there, and untangled the object from an old and decaying fishing net. She pulled the threads away, brushing off sand and detritus from the ocean.

The face of the evil cup looked at her. It was an angry dragon, the cursed thing that had caused so much damage throughout the centuries. Her first urge was to throw the thing into the ocean. But, as it had proven over and over, it would just resurface on this shore, or Albion's shore, or some other shore. It had a life of its own.

This was the first time that she had touched the cup. It had sat upon the mantlepiece of her childhood home. Her brother Ranaulf had taken the cup with him to Caradon Hall. She had *no* desire to touch it, but now she had to if she was going to keep her dog.

"Brendan, we have found it. Here it is, the Enchanted Cup." She placed it into his hands. He moved it around. He remembered the time when he had turned into a sea monster for Ranaulf, and lost five years of his life. And what was the result? The sea was about to crush his boat into matchsticks if he did not throw it back. Yes, this was indeed the cup he remembered. He spontaneously hugged Morag. She hugged him back. The cup, hated as it was, had brought them together. Like most things in life, it was not all bad, not all good. There was a grey area.

They held hands and walked back to their camp. This should have been an extraordinarily happy moment, but it wasn't. It just felt like one step in a journey. Since Brendan was blind, her happiness was gone. They did some hunting and gathering for provisions for the journey home. In the morning, they set sail for Albion.

Chapter Nine

The time passed by slowly, she had to admit. Morag missed her home, her little cottage and her choice of foods. Here on the Cormorant, they ate the same thing every day. Their skin tanned. The sunrises and sunsets were breathtaking, sure, but she still missed Northborough. In a weird way, she missed the community of the Sundays at the Church of the Holy Sandal. She knew that Brendan prayed. He prayed when he woke up and thanked the Lord for another day. He prayed briefly and silently before each meal, saying, "Bless us, oh Lord, and these Thy gifts, which we are about to receive from Thy bounty. Through Christ our Lord, Amen." He prayed when he went to bed at night, kneeling and thanking his Christian God for giving him another day. Was there something to this faith? She could not tell. It really confused her. She felt that if she were *meant* to convert, that she would know it in her heart. But she felt nothing.

Just when she believed that they would make it home in an uneventful manner, up from the roiling sea came a mermaid. She was beautiful, naturally. Aren't all mermaids beautiful? She stood up on her glistening tail of scales and called out to the navigator.

"Captain Brendan! Captain Brendan!"

Brendan became startled and visibly upset. He recognized that voice. He knew that his nemesis, Maeve, was back. And they were so close to making it back to Albion! Back to his normal life. Or, maybe not. He realized that he no longer could patrol the shores for pirates if he could not see. John would need to become the lead coast guard. Now he felt doubly bad. "Morag, it's the mermaid who tortured me all of those years before. What should I do?"

Morag answered that she didn't know; she knew nothing of mermaids. But then Maeve began to sing, and the high-pitched notes hurt their ears. "Okay, okay, Maeve, what do you want this time?" Brendan asked impatiently.

"You know what I want, land-dweller."

Brendan then realized that all that they had done to get the Enchanted Cup was for naught. That Maeve was going to get the cup all along. He became thoughtful and sad. The ship began to rock. The sky darkened to almost black; it looked like night. The first few raindrops fell, then it seemed as though a bucket opened in the sky.

Chapter Ten

"Go inside, Morag!!" Brendan shouted over the din of the storm. But she refused to go.

"No, I'm staying right here with you," she said. She took his hand and placed it upon the steering wheel. "What is going on?" She had to shout over the strident song. The ship lurched and they had to grab on tightly. The sky brightened with a flash of lightning.

"Remember how I told you why my eyes are made of seawater? That a mermaid once wanted to destroy my ship and my men, but I tricked her by throwing a coin that she caught instead? She is back."

"Captain Brendan! I know that you possess the Enchanted Cup of Northborough and I want it back!" Came the voice from down below.

Morag wanted to step in. "Look, you witch. Who do you think you are, actually? You show up in the middle of the ocean and torment this poor, blind man? Forget it, Maeve, I will not throw you the cup back. You can live without it. My dog can't."

Lightning crashed and illuminated the sky again. Maeve seemed to emanate lightning. She was truly scary.

Her hair stood up all around her face. "Did you say *blind*, girl? she asked.

"Yes, of course. Didn't you not know that Brendan went blind trying to save my life by warming me up? Queen Frostleigh froze us; we were surely going to die. But he, being a brave soul, made a bargain. He gave her his ability to change into a sea monster to her. She, living alone on an island, welcomed the chance to explore the world under the sea. But in the exchange, she blinded Brendan, and burned his arms, too. He hears you but cannot see you. So ease up, Maeve. You should pity him, not threaten him."

Brendan again felt small and insignificant. He did *not* want anyone to pity him. He'd had a good life and now had this beautiful girl at his side. But he understood what she was doing, so he said nothing.

"Ha ha, I pity no one! Why should I? But you have given me an idea. Like the exchange you made with my friend Frostleigh, I propose one to you. Simply give me the cup and I will heal your dear Brendan's eyes. What do you say, Morag?"

She thought of Monty, safely inside the cabin. Brendan thought of Monty, too, who was the whole reason for this journey, the reason behind West's death. He called to her, "Absolutely not! No way would I give you the cup. We have been through too much to give it to you now."

But Morag intervened. She squeezed his hand and whispered to him, "Let it be so. I love my doggie Monty, but now I love you, too. Let me do this for you. Who knows? Maybe Cigfa and Branwen won't hurt him. Maybe they were bluffing and only wanted him as a pet. I have to believe this. They can live without the cup. They have lived without it all of these years and they are fine. *Please*, Brendan."

He sadly acknowledged that what she said made sense. Why would the sisters want to hurt Monty anyway? He was a good dog and a perfect companion. Besides, he couldn't imagine the sisters with a mutt. They would want a pure-bred dog, preferably rare breed, surely. He turned his head toward Morag and whispered back, "Okay, but only because I want to spend the rest of my life with you." His heart seemed as if it overgrew the bounds of his chest. He knelt down before her. "I don't have a ring, but will you marry me?"

She cried. She grabbed his chest and pulled him up. They embraced tightly and warmly. Then Morag screamed and screamed, "Yes, yes, yes! I wish the same thing, to live with you forever, captain, my captain. I love you." Despite being blind, Brendan found her mouth, and kissed her.

Chapter Eleven

"What's taking so long for you to answer, land-dweller? I don't have all day. Are you going to accept my generosity or live as a blind man for the rest of your life?"

"You win, Maeve. But how do we know it's not a trick? Give me my sight first. Then we will toss you the cup," he said.

"Do you think I am stupid? Because I have no legs, only a tail, I cannot ascend upon your boat. I am at your mercy here, Captain. What if I healed you and you didn't give me back my price? Let's do this together, on the count of three, all right?"

Brendan wondered why, of all the mermaids in the world, he had to get involved with *this* one. Aren't mermaids supposed to be *nice*? But anxious to get this over with, he agreed.

"One, two, three!" Maeve counted, and Morag threw her the Enchanted Cup. She was glad to get rid of it. She hoped that it would live underwater in some kind of demented museum the mermaid kept there. Maeve caught the cup and disappeared under water, flipping her magnificent teal and purple tail and covering the humans with water. They were soaked. Brendan caught salt water in his eyes and began to rub them vigorously to get the sting out. Then he looked at Morag, really *looked* at her. His eyes were no longer glassy and absent-looking, but they were no longer the color of the sea, either. His eyes shone a clear, green color, like that of the grass covering Northborough. He was healed; he was whole again.

Neither Brendan nor Morag knew why Maeve had wanted the cup so badly. But once they had sailed away, she swam up to the shore of Atlantia, the island where the cup was found. Seawater tasted disgusting, but it was all she had to drink there. "Bottom's up!" she said to herself, hoping that the cup will find a good place for her to start a new life. She wished desperately for a life as a human, with two legs rather than this awful fishy tail. She silently asked the gods to place her somewhere on land, somewhere where a tail would do no good at all. She imagined her new life, tilted her beautiful head back, and drank.

End of Book VIII

Book IX

Regrets for a Princess

Chapter One

Life on the road is never comfortable. It's so much easier to stay home, especially when you live in a castle and have servants who do all the work. When Beatrice moved to Caradon Hall from Wulfgrim Hall, there was not much of a change. But moving to a caravan, well, that was hard for her. Sure, there were handsome horses, and a covered carriage for her to travel in. She enjoyed all of the visits to royal families. It was wonderful to speak with princesses in French, Spanish and Italian. Not that she spoke those languages, but there were translators at each castle. She delighted in tasting the exotic foods in each country. She kind of hated the days when it rained, though. But sunny days were glorious, and she used the time to become closer to Milkolaj.

She wondered about whether her love potion had worked. It didn't really seem like it. While the Pole was friendly and social, she could tell that he was not in love with her. She knew what "in love" looked like. She knew this by the way Mesmin stared at her, the way he would do anything she asked, even things he was wholeheartedly against, like violence and war. She began to doubt her idea to travel with Mikolaj and abandon her family in Northborough.

But here she stayed. It was definitely awkward. He wanted to talk about physics, astronomy and mathematics. She preferred talking about interior design, fashion and parties. It perhaps was not a match made in heaven, but you know what they say, "opposites attract." Still, she was learning about the interior design, fashion and parties of many of the royals of Europe, and she had some great ideas to try out once home in Northborough!

Chapter Two

She felt glad when they finally made their way through Genoa, nearing Rome. Bea could feel the weather warming up and improving. But then Mikolaj became sick. It began with his feeling weak and lethargic. He developed a fever, and Bea became concerned. She sought out a doctor. The doctor examined him, noticing the enlarged lymph nodes in his neck, armpits and groin. The doctor quickly left after being paid, saying that a new disease had been going around, one that might become quite serious.

The next day Mikolaj felt worse. He complained of stomach pain and stopped eating. Then he experienced chills, and parts of his body turned black. Be took him to the local priest, not knowing what else to do. Her servants carried him into their carriage and then to the local church.

Old Padre Francesco looked concerned. He wanted to help this young man, but he had seen this disease before. He tried to talk to Mikolaj.

"Son, can you hear me? I am a priest."

"Can't you cure him?" screeched Bea. "Wasn't your leader a miracle-worker? What's wrong with you! He's dying!"

It seemed as though the young man was. His skin became more and more black, with lumps in it.

"Dear lady, I am just a parish priest. You are correct. Our leader, Jesus Christ, did many miraculous things. He healed people. He fed thousands from five loaves and two fish. He cured lepers and brought a dead man, his friend Lazarus, back to life. He came back from the dead! But no one can stop this horrific pestilence."

It looked like Mikolaj wanted to speak.

Bea leaned down close to him and put her ear by his mouth. She wanted to kiss him but knew that would be inappropriate. "What is it dear?" Bea asked.

"Pre...preserve my i...ideas. Do not allow them to die with me. Take my theory to Rome. The truth...the truth...must..." were his final words. His body stopped moving and his lovely eyes stared straight up. Mikolaj was dead.

Chapter Three

Bea tried to cry over his body and to hug him, but Padre Francesco pulled her away. "You must not touch him. This pestilence spreads rapidly and it is deadly. We do not know how it spreads, but the humours and airs surrounding the body are sure to infect you, and then all whom you contact. Save yourself, lady, and stay away."

She didn't want to seem as though she did not love him, but perhaps she didn't. Maybe this was all a fascination, an infatuation for the new and different. She hated herself. She really did. She wanted to scream and throw things. She wanted to hit someone. How could she have been so stupid? She had a husband at home who loved her more than the sun.

"UUUUUUUUGGGGGGHHHHH!" she cried.

If only Mesmin were here, her dear Mesmie. He would have saved the mathematician. He possessed great powers, obviously greater than the simple priest's. At that moment she realized how much she loved and missed her husband, and sobbed. The priest thought that she cried over Mikolaj, but that was not so. After all, she'd just met him and he was almost certainly insane. Who says the earth revolves around the sun?

When she had calmed down, she spoke to Padre Francesco about burying Mikolaj, who followed his faith. "Just do whatever you normally do." She didn't care anymore. Suddenly, all she wanted to do was get away, and *fast*. She was not about to travel further south to another city and expose herself to more disease. She gave orders to her servants to pack everything and turn the hoses around to head north, home, to Northborough.

Chapter Four

Morvan sulked around the castle, feeling melancholy and not engaged in leadership. He allowed the Order of the New Pegasus to take care of the court's business of ruling. Sir Ranaulf naturally fell into the role of leader, so Morvan did not worry. However, his girlfriend looked at him as if he were the enemy. Would she ever marry him as long as his moodiness persisted?

The dreams would not stop. They invaded his sleep with frightening scenes of murder. He was his father's son. He resembled his dad in more ways than appearance, dreading violence and anything to do with blood. But he kept thinking that this Mikolaj deserved to die. Look what the astrologer has done to his father! Mesmin had been so happy to be married to Beatrice. The day he won her hand at the St. John's Day tournament was a triumph for him. He had not meant to burn the king's arm, he really hadn't. Mesmin was just so focused on winning the Beatrice the Fair, the prize. Where had that victorious man gone? Hiding in his room, drowning his sadness with vino since his wife had left him for a stranger.

The worst thing happened the other day. He was so ashamed. Ophelia had come to him with his midday meal. She poured some tea and sat down next to him. She tried to make conversation about the weather, usually a safe subject. "It's so nice how the warmth of the sun brings us out of winter. I love to watch the bulbs on the trees open, the cherry and apple blossoms perfume the air, don't you, Morvan?"

He looked at her with disgust, and his arm just flew to her face on its own. He hadn't meant to. It just happened. How could she think of things like spring buds and sunshine when his father, cuckolded by his mother, drank away his sorrow? He loved them both so much and his mind went in different directions, like his arms being stretched and pulled. *Oh no,* he thought, *I have struck her in the face.*

Ophelia looked shocked. She thought of her former life as a barmaid, and how her boss had never hit her. But she knew that she could not go back there, as she was now entangled with the most powerful man in Northborough, and he would find her. She lightly touched her face. It was red and swollen. It felt as if it were on fire.

Chapter Five

"Ophelia, Oh, my Ophelia! I am so sorry! Can you ever forgive me? I didn't mean to. I--I haven't been getting a lot of sleep lately, and just am not myself. You know that, right, darling? You know that I am not violent. It will never happen again, I promise. I have been plagued by nightmares, and cannot sleep. You know, I've told you, all about my haunting. And your face, your beautiful face is precious to me. I could not mar it! Oh, no, what have I done? Please, dear, tell me you are all right!" pleaded Morvan, truly abhorring his action.

Ophelia picked up her head from her hands. She knew that she had to play his game here. She wasn't born yesterday. She was dealing with a king. One thing about human nature, she had learned was that it did not change. It is said: "The tiger does not change his stripes." If he has hit her once, he will never stop. She will be trapped, trapped for the rest of her life in an abusive relationship. She had seen women in this situation before, and there was no way she would allow herself to be ensnared like an animal, serving and smiling, when behind closed doors she was being slapped or worse. Then, when the children came...it was too much to contemplate. She touched her raw, burning cheek. Then she looked up at Morvan, the young man she once desired.

"I'm fine, my love. Of course, it was nothing. You are under so much stress right now. I am sure everything will work out; don't worry," she said.

"But what about you? Can you ever forgive me?"

"You have already been forgiven. I understand how you feel. It is terrible how your mum has left your poor dad all alone, a laughingstock of the borough. I feel so badly for him, but myself, I am fine. I know that you're a good man, and I could never find a better man."

Haltingly, slowly, he moved toward her. He looked at her with questioning eyes, asking permission of the lowly barmaid for a hug. She opened her arms to him and they embraced, warmly. She practiced her deep breathing technique, where the measured breaths automatically calmed her and slowed down her heart. Closing her eyes, she allowed the human closeness. Could she stop the wedding plans? Could Branwen and Cigfa's efforts to beautify her and orchestrate the wedding of the decade come to naught? She thought carefully.

Chapter Six

Bea always tried to look her best. No stringy hair for her! Her hair needed to shine, something not always easy with waves. Her face needed to look as flawless as a baby's bottom, soft as a cloud and unblemished. Her eye makeup looked like powdered jewels had landed upon her lids, like artistic black lines painted from the brush of an artist. Her clothes, as suiting a royal family member, cost more than a peasant earns in a year. She needed furs to keep her warm as she traveled. The finest lace, crocheted in Gaul, adorned her neck and cuffs. The heaviest velvet formed her dresses, no common cotton or wool for a former princess and queen mother. The velvet had been double-woven from silk, and no one else she knew owned any. Strings of pearls looped around her elegant neck. These pearls came from the East. Naturally, she had stayed slim. Needless to say, her hair was perfectly coiffed into rolls of deep red woven into a crown made from more pearls. Despite being on the road for weeks, she thought that she was ready to make her entrance, or re-entrance, back into Northborough.

The whispers began right away. "There she is…it's Beatrice and she is *alone*!" they said. "Oh, look, but don't be seen a-lookin' as it's the Queen Mother riding her horse but without the Gothic stranger by her side. He must have tired of her," they murmured.

She knew they would gossip. That is what people did. No bother, she held her head high. No one could say anything against the Queen Mother. Her son was a good king. Had he not just held a wonderful banquet for May Day? She would have to ask him about that. Her first stop was to see her son again. But then, the inevitable. She must go back to Mesmin. She must see if there is any chance at all for forgiveness. She felt tired, however. More like exhausted. Breath was coming only with difficulty. So she traveled to Caradon Hall, where she could sleep in her own bed again, such a relief after all of the different ones she'd rested her head in over this long, sad journey.

Chapter Seven

Godfrey admitted her and politely asked about her trip. He took her mount and let the groom stable, water and feed him. The groom would brush the horse's coat and check his shoes for wear. Bea never had to worry about transportation. But she felt anxious and the anxiety led to nervousness. Her ladies fussed over her arrival. They led her upstairs to her solar, where she promptly fainted.

"Princess! Princess!" The ladies all cooed and called to her. In the depth of her consciousness she began to hear them but just blacked out again. A healer was called for, who passed strong smelling salts over her nose, and she began to awaken. Her alabaster skin appeared paler than ever. They worried that she may have hit her head as she fell. "Can you hear me?" a voice slowly came into her head. It was a familiar voice, a voice close to her heart.

Morvan leaned over the body of his mother. He noticed that she had blackish lumps appearing on her beautiful skin. This was not a good sign. "Morvan, my dearest, please call for my husband," she whispered. To her ladies, she said, "I perspire; please change my garments into summer ones." Morvan ran to Godfrey and told him to summon Mesmin post haste. "NOW!" he shouted. *"NOW!"* he said again.

He ran back to his mother. He gently wiped the wisps of hair from her face, which had fallen when her crown came off. "Mother, mother, what is it?" he called to her. Her brain felt foggy and she could not remember. She felt so warm, so very uncomfortable. All of a sudden she lacked the power to get up and go to her bed, so they carried her there. They offered her some chamomile tea, which she accepted but did not drink.

Chapter Eight

Mesmin loved his wife. He always had. It was instant infatuation from the moment he saw her. From that glimpse, there was no other woman for him. His powers meant that he could make any woman fall in love with him, but what was the satisfaction in that? He wanted to be wanted. He was pretty sure that all people wanted to be wanted.

They had such a nice life together at Wulfgrim Hall. They got along so well. Everything was fine until that stranger appeared and ruined everything. Now they had summoned him. He never wanted to see Mikolaj again. He was certain that if he did, he would cast some horrible spell upon the astrologer. It would be too easy. It had taken all of his effort not to do so before, but he knew he had to let Beatrice go and find her own heart.

For fortification, he took a large gulp of the wine he was enjoying at the moment. *Why not?* He said to himself, and corked the bottle, carrying it under his arm. He hurried along to Caradon Hall, where Bea, according to the messenger, lay terribly sick.

He was led to her room. There was no sign of Mikolaj. Her skin was a ghostly white; her eyes vacant. In a cold, cold voice, he said to her, "Yes? You called for me?" He knew it was cold. How else was he supposed to feel? Not only having been shamed, he was also devastated.

"Mesmin, my dearest. I'm so sorry. I have embarrassed you and never, ever should have left Albion with that man. I am completely at fault. I don't know if you can ever forgive me, but I am asking your forgiveness from the bottom of my heart. You have always been there for me. You always gave me every little and big thing I asked of you. Your heart is bigger than this castle, bigger than the sky. Look at me, this pitiful creature, whose heart is the size of a beetle's. I am not worthy of your love, but I ask only for your forgiveness, as I feel that my time here on this earth fades away."

By this point the tears cascaded down from his worried face. He wished he were not such a pushover, but pushover he was. Even through the alcohol, he felt his heart melt. "But Beatrice, where is he? Where is the stranger?"

"*Dead!* He died in Italy as he made his way to Rome with his ridiculous theory. And I'm glad! As if he could convince the Church that the earth revolved around the sun! I was so wrong to follow him; I don't know what came over me. You are my only love; the only one I have ever loved. Please forgive me, Mesmie!"

Mesmin bent down close to her. He kissed her softly on her cheek. "Of course I forgive you, you silly woman. I love you more than life. Now rest, and get over this illness quickly, so that we can return to our lives together."

She closed her eyes. That was all that she needed to hear. The pain grew within her; she had never felt so tired. *So, at least something has been salvaged.* Her sweet husband had forgiven her. Bea reflected on her life. The thrilling tournament, the birth of her son and his coronation. These are the things that had been emblazoned upon her heart. *I'll just take a little nap*, she said to herself.

End of Book IX

Book X

A Chance for Happiness

Chapter One

Morvan ran back to his mother's room. The ladies had called him frantically. *"Please come soon!* She is dying!" they screeched at him. And he ran. He was young and fit. But when he arrived, he knew it was too late. His mother's placid face had lost its beauty due to this cursed disease. Lumps had formed on her neck. The lumps were turning an unattractive shade of purple-black. His head hurt to see her looking like this. "Mum? Mum?" he called. But there was no answer. He feared touching her neck for a pulse, so he held her wrist, hoping to feel the rush of blood. But there was none.

Morvan lay next to his mother. Here was his first home. She had nurtured him, smiled at his first accomplishments, planned all of his birthdays. Naturally, the nurses had actually taken care of him and raised him, fed him and washed his clothes, but Beatrice was the one who lit the way with her beauty, charm, and competence. She knew how to arrange things. She knew the *right* way to do things. Even as King of Northborough, he was so proud of her.

Except of course when the stranger arrived and she became infatuated with him. The one who haunted his dreams. Now he no longer needed to plan the man's execution, since gratefully he was already dead. Maybe of the same disease to which his mother had succumbed. A troubling thought went through his mind. What if his mother had brought this disease to Northborough? There was no way to tell but to wait. Hopefully it was just something they had contracted, some bad humours, on the road. But as the ruler of the kingdom, he was responsible for the health of everyone. It was time for the New Order of the Pegasus to meet.

CHAPTER TWO

It came to Sir George to go though Beatrice's things when it became clear that she would no longer need them. He walked to the stables and found her handsome horse alone and just chewing on some hay. "Click click," he made a sound with his lips, and he went to the knight. George pet him and gave him a little piece of carrot as a treat. Then he began to unpack the saddle bags of the queen mother's things.

One by one, he handed to Sir Douglas her clothing, boots, jewelry and coats. Then he came upon a curious item, a vial which contained a tiny amount of a sweet-smelling liquid, just at the bottom. The label on the vial read,

Venenum.

That is strange, he thought. It sounds like "venom" or snake poison. What can it be? He sipped the rest of it. Well, it sure doesn't taste like venom. Then he thought about that, and realized that he had never tasted venom. *Either way, I think it's harmless,* he reasoned. The next odd thing that he found was a little doll in the form of a statue of a woman, crafted from silver. She had crystal blue stones for eyes, and a cord ran through her neck.

Just then he turned to look at Sir Douglas. He felt an inexplicable emotion. He felt nauseous and a spinning stomach. George reached for Douglas' hand, but Douglas turned away. "Sorry, mate," said Sir George. "I don't know what came over me. Just a little emotional, that's it."

"No worries, mate," said Douglas, uncomfortably. What had happened to the knight at the head of the round table? "We best show this to Mesmin, though. Bring him her personal effects." They didn't know what the doll was. But Mesmin would.

"Right. Good idea. Let's go."

Chapter Three

Mesmin sat in his room with his bottle of wine as a candle slowly made its way down the wick. So his beloved wife was dead. He had some mixed feelings about that. He couldn't stop the love that kept bubbling up from his heart, despite how she had betrayed him. And he knew that all she had in life were himself and their son. Her sister Catherine and her brother Rory had left this world before her. He heard a knock at his door.

"Come in," he said.

Sir George and Sir Douglas arrived, carrying all of Beatrice's things from the journey. "Where would you like these, Mesmin?" asked George.

The sorcerer looked up from his cup. He could use a spell to make all of her things disappear, and he was about to when...he saw something glint in the sunshine. It was the eyes of the doll. The aquamarine eyes of the little amulet. He sighed and felt terribly sad. His wife had used a love charm to entice the stranger. Now he felt even worse than before. He pointed at the pile of things in Douglas' arms and called out,

Douglas was left holding nothing. Mesmin thought about using the spell on Bea's body, but there was no point.

She had gone. A complicated woman, she was a warm and loving mother, but so obsessed with power that it had blinded her to living a happy and fulfilled life. She always wanted more, and one who always wants more can never rest. He hoped that she rested now.

A messenger arrived, asking to speak to the two knights. They asked if they should take their leave, but Mesmin said it was all right to speak there. The messenger hesitated as he did not want to further burden Mesmin, but spoke as ordered. "Sir George and Sir Douglas, the fair lady Ophelia has not been in the castle since yesterday. She did not sleep in her bed. The king asks you and the rest of the knights to find her as he fears for her safety." Worried, the two knights left as quickly as they could after saying goodbye to the sorcerer.

Mesmin was wondering, *what next?* His beloved son had finally found someone to love, and now she had gone missing. He hoped that she was feeling well. He himself was not. In fact, he walked over to his bed and lay down. It was quite hot in his room and he struggled to breathe.

Chapter Four

"Quickly, hurry up!" shouted Sir George as he assembled his knights. They mounted their horses but spread out in order to find Ophelia. He himself rode to the tavern, thinking she may have gone back to her old life. He could not understand why, since women were mysteries to him. In her old life she was a barmaid; in her new life she was a queen-to-be, with luxurious clothes, new jewels, hair and makeup from Cigfa and Branwen, and a wedding to look forward to. But perhaps she simply wanted to see her old friends again.

The other knights spread out over the countryside. Dogs were brought in, smelling some of her clothes to get her scent. Sir Douglas followed one of the hounds to a river. He dismounted and walked to the shore, looking down into the shallow water. It smelled of fresh rain and the blossoms of May. A beautiful gown moved with the current, a gown of layers of gossamer gold lace over burnished bronze. Ophelia's lovely face, swollen and pale, lay motionless, her eyes, blank.

Flowers of magenta and white dotted the riverbank here and there. Deep green ferns grew along the edge. Marshes stood next to the lifeless body. It looked as though she had been holding a red rose before she succumbed to the water. Even in death, she was so pulchritudinous that she took his breath away.

He blew a horn and his fellows arrived, silently taking in the scene. Without a word, they pulled her out and lay her body upon one of the horses, and led her to Caradon Hall. Sir George hoped it was an accident, for that is how it would be explained to the people and to Brother Bede. Suicides were not allowed to be buried in the church graveyard. But he knew that his duty was to bring her to Morvan first, so that is where they went.

It was Morvan who let the ladies-in-waiting know that Ophelia had gone missing. He had a bad feeling about this. He wondered if it had been her reaction to his violence. Could she have run away? But surely she knew she would be found. *Ah,* he thought. *She probably just needed a break from me.* Pre-wedding jitters are a common problem.

Chapter Five

While he waited for the Knights of the New Order of the Pegasus to bring his fiancee home, another couple had arrived. *The Cormorant,* riding the winds created by Branwen and Cigfa, had already anchored on Albion's coast. As soon as it stopped on the beach, the gangplank descended and Brendan and Morag ran to their home soil, bending and kissing the ground. Then they tumbled and kissed each other with sandy mouths, laughing at nothing and everything. Monty barked and jumped with joy.

Morag inhaled the salty smell of her own land, the fish and the mussels and all of the seafood odors put together. It was *so* good to be home. Brendan ran to her and they held each other closely. It had been a perilous journey, and ostensibly pointless as they still didn't have the Enchanted Cup, but they had each other. Brendan's arms were burned and full of ugly scarring, but she could care less. She wanted to gaze into his eyes all day.

They made their way toward the castle, where they would have to give a report to King Morvan about his

Morvanland. They planned to tell him that indeed, the land to the west was now named after him. But he would not see them.

So they walked, hand-in-hand, toward Morag's cottage. Brendan never had a home as he had lived his whole life on the ship. He hoped that John had not encountered any issues while patrolling Albion's coast in his new boat.

Not terribly surprisingly, Cigfa, the lilac lady, and Branwen, the green witch, waited for them there. Morag startled and lost her breath for a moment. Brendan understood the situation when he watched his fianccée's reaction.

"I see you have made it back safely," said Cigfa in a menacing tone.

"And the little mutt as well," chimed in Branwen.

"So just hand over the cup and we'll be on our way," Cigfa demanded.

"Now just a moment," said Captain Brendan in his most commanding voice. "You have no right to this dog. He has been Morag's her whole life. We had the Cup, we did, but then Maeve the Mermaid wanted it back." He rolled up his sleeves. "Look at my arms. Look at how I have been burned in our quest for the cup. If we had it, we would give it to you, but we don't have it. I'm sorry but we have failed. Why does it matter to you anyway?"

"Look, it's none of your business," said Branwen, as Monty flew up into the air and started circling around them. On his face was a look of desperation.

Morag felt sick in her stomach and began to cry. Brendan couldn't bear to hear her cry. "Ladies, what can we do for you? We don't have the Cup. After all of this sailing and encountering magic and witchcraft, we have nothing to show for it. What could we give you in exchange?"

Cigfa grinned. This was better than she ever imagined. "Ha ha, it's no problem, Captain. Have your stupid mutt back." Monty gently fell onto the ground. Morag cried and ran to him, hugging and crying at the same time.

Branwen knew what her sister was thinking. "It's obvious to anyone that you two are in love. All we ask is your first child be given to us. A dog for a child, that's fair, right?"

Morag now looked horrified. *No!* she thought. *That is not a fair exchange at all!* But it was done the moment she had accepted her dog in her arms. Morag tried to put this out of her mind. The purple and olive women disappeared. In their place was a bunch of lavender tied with a beautiful green silk ribbon.

Chapter Six

When the knights brought Ophelia to Morvan, he was inconsolate. He slammed doors; he threw vases and goblets. He screamed his loudest insults at the gods for doing this to him. This was to hide his inner terror that it was really his fault. He kissed her dull forehead; he brushed her wet hair from her dear face. Oh, the pain! How would he ever recover from this?

At the same time he felt very weak. Then, he noticed how hot it was in the room. He removed his royal robe and then started removing other layers. Off came the tights and the vest, leaving only his plain oatmeal-colored wool tunic. Even so, he still felt too warm. He had to lay down. Sir

George noticed the lumps forming upon his body, all over his body. He knew from Beatrice's body that these would turn black and that his highness did not have much longer to live.

"Knights, what can we do to save our king?" he asked, because Morvan had been a good king and he loyally served him. Sir Douglas mentioned that this very disease was ravaging the countryside. People were dying in the fields, at home, on the road. They were using wheelbarrows to carry the dead. Brother Bede had become overwhelmed with funerals.

George wished that Gondebald were around. He would know what to do! He hurried up to Mesmin's room, but Mesmin was dead. So he ran, full-speed toward the church, to ask Brother Bede. He was at wit's end. His king could not die. Who would succeed him? the country would be thrown into chaos with the entire royal family gone. The Gauls, or worse, the Vikings or the Celts might take over.

Outside of the Church, he spotted little Goslar, selling holy dirt. The elf looked rosy and robust; living at the church had brought him back to health. Goslar called out to him, "Sir, try the dirt! It can't hurt!"

"What do you mean, 'Try the dirt?'"? he wondered.

"I have seen them bringing in the bodies. Nothing seems to stop this plague of death. But perhaps my holy dirt will. After all, it is composed partly of the Holy Sandal worn by Our Lord Himself."

"How does it work?"

"Just take some and mix it with water. Put it on the lumps in the skin of the suffering victim. It's worth a try."

"I feel very foolish purchasing dirt, but I am desperate. How much for the dirt?"

"I am glad you asked because I have a special today. Usually one bucket will cost you three pence, but today I will sell it for two."

"And what do you do with this money?"

"I give it to brother Bede for hosting me. It goes to the Church, Sir George."

"You are a good elf, and, as you say, it cannot hurt. People are dying so fast. I will purchase a bucket, and if it helps, I will buy some more!"

George handed Goslar some money, and took the bucket. "Thank you and talk to you soon, Goslar. I have to hurry!"

Goslar waved goodbye, not even aware of just how urgent the knight's mission was.

Chapter Seven

Brendan woke up to the smell of delicious food cooking. Morag was baking an oat cake and grilling some meat. She happily hummed to herself, when Brendan snuck up behind her and gave her a bear hug encircling her tiny waist. Monty watched the scene from a rug on the floor, and when he saw how happy his two parents were, his tail thumped rhythmically.

"Would you like some tea?" she asked.

Brendan yawned and nodded his assent. This new life was almost too good to be true. He had never felt so content. He supposed that soon, he would have to go back to his old job, patrolling the shores of Northborough. But he was in no hurry. Life was good.

"You know, Brendan, you're not going to boss me around once we are married."

"Dear, of course I know that. You have a strong personality and I would never want you to change."

"So I was wondering how you felt about my writing out our marriage vows."

"What?" he gulped, "isn't that already scripted by the Church?" This was their first experience of disagreement! He felt frightened. He wanted to be in control, but he did not want to displease his fiancee.

"Brendan, you know that I am not a Christian."

"But...I always thought I'd be married in a church. I mean, I would *like* to be married in a church."

"But I never envisioned marriage at all, let alone by some religious patriarchy."

"Can we compromise on this? Perhaps Mesmin could officiate alongside Brother Bede. What do you think?"

"Yes, I like that idea. But where would we hold the ceremony?"

"Why not on the beach? You are a captain, after all. You love the sea, right?"

Brendan had to think about this a little. It was highly irregular to get married on a beach with a sorcerer officiating. But he wanted to please Morag so much. They had been through a lot together. His parents and her parents were both gone, so they could not object. He *had* loved the sea until recently, until their journey to America, or Morvanland, or whatever it was called. The encounters with Maeve and Queen Frostleigh had taken a lot out of him. He no longer felt the same.

"Let me just ask Brother Bede, and if he agrees, but I think it's a splendid idea." He didn't *really* think that, but did not want to disappoint her. It was the first little white lie of their relationship. Brendan did not realize that after telling one lie, the rest would come more easily, driving a notch between them.

Chapter Eight

Brendan went to find Brother Bede, but he found pandemonium instead. Morag would not stay home, so she saw the spread of terminal illness all around her. She wished that she had magical powers, so that she could just make the disease go away. Since she did not, she told Brendan that she was taking up residence at St. Bathilde's to care for the sick. Some died before they even made it to the hospital, but she cared for those suffering with the sisters.

Some people did not catch the disease. No one understood why. But those that it touched, it killed within days. Doctors could not explain it. Sorcerers could not cure it. So Morag only hoped to provide a caring face and words to those at the hospital. She brought them water, washed their sweating faces, and carried them outside with the help of a nun when they passed away.

Meanwhile, Sir George arrived at the castle. He jumped off his mount and ran, carrying the bucket of dirt, feeling rather silly. But he had to give it a try. Godfrey opened the door and got out of his way. George ran to the king's room, and screamed, "Get me some water!"

Water was brought and he mixed it with the dirt, forming a thick paste. The king groaned in pain, he was losing consciousness. Sir George spoke to him as he applied the salve, "My liege, I am just putting some medicine upon your sores. I think it will help you." Morvan muttered something indistinguishable. It seemed as if he had fallen asleep.

But then...no...could it be? A miracle occurred. The sores became smaller, and went back to skin tone. So the little elf was right! Morvan began to turn his head left and right. The putrid smell receded and he smelled good again. The king opened his eyes. "Where am I?" he wondered.

"Sire! You are in your room at Caradon Hall! You have been gravely ill but are better now! However, the entire kingdom is suffering from this unknown disease and I need to get more of this salve to help them!"

"You are a good knight. Go and do what you have to. Thank you--and I will never forget this. You will be rewarded." With that, Sir George took his leave.

Chapter Nine

Sir George hurried to the stable, where his horse had been brushed, fed and watered, and asked for him back. He called out to Sir Douglas. "Douglas, get the rest of the Knights of the New Order of the Pegasus and tell them to purchase all of the dirt being sold by Goslar. He is at the Church. When the dirt is mixed with water, it forms a paste that cures this pestilence. Hurry!"

George himself rushed ahead and brought buckets and buckets of the dirt to St. Bathildes. Goslar set about digging more dirt. You never know, he thought, when something might become useful. He had a feeling, and he was right. His business was thriving, not because he wanted people to be sick, but because he wanted to help. They had thought he sold something like snake oil, a fake relic. But while poor souls throughout Europe died of this mysterious disease, most of Northborough would be spared.

After a couple of weeks the fear was over, and the disease disappeared. There were the usual diseases, coughing, sniffling, fever here and there. There were the broken bones and the madness. Influenza, arthritis, leprosy, lice and seizures. But the horrible, swift death-dealing illness was gone. At Mass that Sunday, the people cheered Goslar. "Hurray for Goslar!" they called out, and he turned red with embarrassment. He was just glad to help. Afterwards, Brendan approached Brother Bede.

"A wedding on the beach? Are you kidding, lad?" he asked.

"It's my fiancee's wish, Father. You know what they say, 'Happy wife, happy life.'"

"Well, I had not heard that before, but it makes sense. I have seen many couples, and the happier ones are the ones where the husband is considerate and thoughtful of his wife. For, as the apostle Paul said,

'Husbands, love your wives...Even so husbands should love their wives as their own bodies. He who loves his wife loves himself. For no man ever hates his own flesh, but nourishes and cherishes it, as Christ does the church, because we are members of his body. "For this reason a man shall leave his father and mother and be joined to his wife, and the two shall become one."'

Furthermore, why not have the celebration on the beach? That way there will be no overcrowding. Shall we perform the vows next Saturday?"

"I have to ask 'the boss,' but please plan for it. Neither of us has a family, but the whole of Northborough is invited! I will provide a feast, but perhaps you could spread the word?"

"Consider it done, good Captain, consider it done."

Chapter Ten

"I've never felt so happy," said Morag. She looked ravishing, with her braids in a knot on top of her head, and her makeup done by Cigfa and Branwen. When the sisters found out that there was to be a wedding, they jumped right into their new role of wedding planners. C&B Weddings was booked for a year in advance, now that they were doing this huge occasion. Morag's gown was pure white, with little seed pearls woven into it. The simple dress was long, with a long train. Her gossamer veil was long as well, covering her face for now. C&B Weddings had designed the gown and simply conjured it. There were no more warlocks left in Northborough, so their services as witches were much in demand. As much as they were saddened by the death of

Ophelia and the chance to organize a royal wedding, this one was more fun.

After all, never had a Christian wedding been performed outside of a church in their borough. How exciting! Sadly, Mesmin was going to perform the rites along with Brother Bede, but he had perished. Giles stepped in his place. Morag wrote her own vows in the form of a poem. Scandalous! What would women ask for next? Equal rights? A great crowd formed in the sand. They had all removed their shoes and sandals. Music provided a festive atmosphere.

Bede had never seen so many flowers. There were flowers everywhere, and the scent was both intoxicating and wonderful. Cigfa and Branwen had made them appear by magic, looking like they had been cut that morning. He wore his nicest robes. Nerves overtook his body, but some wine helped with that. This was a first for him. All of the people of Northborough *needed* a happy occasion. Every family had been touched by death from the mysterious disease. And while the disease had disappeared, people were wary and afraid. They believed that Beatrice had brought the terrible sickness from Italy. That meant that any stranger could bring more disease. Life was so precious, but so fleeting. They wanted to have some fun and celebrate, and live in the moment for a change. So they left their fields, their animals, their shops and butcheries, their taverns and silversmiths, and gathered together.

Chapter Eleven

Gentle music played in the background. In time with the lute, Bede began, "Captain Brendan, do you take Morag to be your wife?"

"I do," he responded.

"Do you promise to love and care

In old age and youth,

Always telling the truth,

Do you promise to listen

When she talks,

Do you promise to cuddle

And go for long walks,

when times are good,

And when times are tough,

Do you promise to console her

And tell her she is enough?

Do you promise to respect her

Forsaking all others,

And finally, until death do you part,

Do you promise to give her

Every bit of your heart?"

"I do." He reached over to her hand, and placed a golden ring decorated with Celtid knots on her finger. C & B Weddings had seen to this important detail!

There was not a dry eye on the beach. Everyone's eyes teared up. Morag had written a simple and beautiful poem. The wind blew her dress away from her feet. Between the smell of the flowers, the music, and his beautiful wife, Brendan's heart felt as if it were breaking.

Morag answered the traditional vows, read by Giles, "I do."

"Brendan and Morag, I now pronounce you *husband* and wife. You may kiss *each other*." Morag lifted her veil. More passionately than they should, they went right ahead.

Coming up for air, Brendan looked into the crowd. He could not believe it. There, standing on two legs, was Maeve. He did not know it, but the magic in the cup, by placing her on solid ground, had also granted her two legs and removed her tail. It had brought her to Northborough, of all places! Seeing her again really shook him up. But he resolved to put her out of his mind. Today was his wedding day!

Bede, who was standing next to Giles, held his friend's hand. He looked into Giles' beautiful copper eyes. "Do you think there may be a day when we can get married, too?" he asked.

Giles, who was, after all, a seer, whispered back, "I see it happening, but not in our lifetimes, friend. It will take hundreds of years."

"I will wait for you," he replied.

"And I for you."

The End

Made in the USA
Middletown, DE
23 August 2020